# TEMPTED BY FIRE

*Blood Oath #2*

## J.A. CARTER

# ALSO BY J.A. CARTER

*Blood Oath Series*
*Bound in Crimson*
*Tempted by Fire*
*Entangled in Scarlet*
*Fated in Ruby*
*Unraveled by Desire*

# BLURB

**We'll burn this city to the ground to find her.**

Taken by one enemy and held captive by another, Calla is forced deeper into the supernatural world of power games and deceit, used in a vicious attempt to gain leverage over the vampires she's bound to. But she isn't about to be a pawn —not again.

Haunted by his dark and bloody past, Gabriel may have no choice but to reunite with the woman from his nightmares to get Calla back, while Atlas, Kade, and Lex are left to deal with the vampire hunters, an age-old threat that has made a deadly, modern-day comeback.

When Calla finally gets the answers she's been searching for and discovers there are more dangerous things than the men she wants to hate but her body craves, she must face the reality that letting herself care about them only gives her more to lose. And with enemies closing in on all sides, she could lose everything.

*For you, the reader.*

## GABRIEL

I don't consider myself a particularly violent person.

Despite being a vampire, that has never been my nature. But the moment I knew Calla was gone, an unfamiliar sensation sparked deep in my chest. Something dark and vicious. It threatens to replace the taste of her on my lips. Her sweet skin and rich blood. Two memories I'd never wish to part with.

A quick search of the house—the paper scattered on the floor in Atlas's office and the obvious decoy note in the kitchen—told us all we needed to know.

Calla had run.

What it didn't explain was why none of us could sense her anymore.

I'd been at work planning a new campaign for our senate candidate when the connection fizzled out. Like blowing out a candle in a dark room, quickly fading smoke is the only remnant of the flame that once burned brightly inside. One moment she was there, and the next, I couldn't feel her at all. Where there was once a vibrating orb of warmth in my chest

—the connection each of us has to her blood—was replaced by a cold emptiness that made me shudder.

Before I could contact any of the guys, Kade called me, confirming what I already knew—something had happened to Calla. Not long after, Brighton Ellis reached out looking for her, saying that she was waiting for Calla to come over but she never showed up.

While Atlas and Lex got on a flight back to the city from JFK in New York, Kade and I started searching. We couldn't locate Calla, but we were able to track her phone to where it was left on the sidewalk outside of Brighton's apartment building, the screen shattered.

Kade had stared at it for a long stretch of silence, focused on the fragmented background image of Calla and Brighton with their arms around each other as they smiled at the camera, with the Washington Monument in the background. I wanted to comfort him. Kade's like a brother to me, and he was there through some of my worst years. While he doesn't know the extent of the darkness in me, he never let me go through that shit alone.

I took the phone from his hands, and the hardness in his eyes as he looked at me did nothing but fuel the fire in my chest to get our girl back.

After a brief conversation, Brighton showed us the texts she'd received from Calla.

*Brighton, we need to talk.*

*I have to tell you some crazy things that won't make much sense, but I promise I'm telling the truth.*

*Please answer me. I'm freaking out over here.*

*Where are you? I'll come to you.*

*Brighton?!?!*

"I don't understand," Brighton told us, wrapping her arms around herself as her hazel eyes shifted back and forth between us. "She was so panicked, then she just stopped responding to me and never showed up. I... I didn't know who else to call. Calla's family is in New York, and you guys seem to be close to her, and I... I have to admit, I'm freaking out."

Kade and I exchanged a quick glance before he glamoured her to delete everything and forget Calla had texted her. The last thing we needed was the Ellis family sticking their noses into this. We had enough to deal with when it came to them as it was. *Damn vampire hunters...*

"Gabe, did you hear what I said?"

Marcel's deep voice pulls me back to the present, to the sitting room of his Manhattan townhouse. The narrow rooms with tall ceilings are decorated with art pieces he's collected over the years. The space is accented with dark blues and grays, glossy hardwood floors, with the smell of leather furniture and crisp citrus candles, which he seems to have burning in every room. It's a bit overwhelming for my senses, but I do my best to ignore the dull ache it's creating in my temples.

I blink at our informant, one of the few people we trust outside the four of us, then force a nod. "Apologies," I mutter.

He rakes a hand through his mop of golden blond hair and sighs. "I get it, man. You're worried about her. But it's only been a week, and—"

"Just tell me what you know, Marcel," I cut him off.

He offers a curt nod, not at all thrown off by my cool tone. "First thing's first. There have been no further developments where Dante is concerned."

My upper lip curls at the mention of him—the vampire who believes he has some claim to what is *ours* because he got screwed out of a job when Calla's ancestor agreed to our protection in exchange for her.

"The guy has gone radio silent," Marcel continues. "I had a friend check out some of the places he's been known to frequent, but he hasn't been around in a while. It's safe to say he's not in New York."

A muscle ticks along my jaw, and I grip the armrest tighter. "Then where the hell is he?" The words taste bitter on my tongue, like drinking stale blood.

Marcel just stares at me, his silver eyes dark, focused. We're both thinking the same thing—the bastard went to Washington. "Let's think about this," he says in a level voice, drumming his fingers against his jean-clad thigh. "We know Dante. He's into the whole pomp and circumstance. If he took Calla, don't you think you'd know about it by now? For the sole reason that the jackass doesn't know how to keep his mouth shut. He'd want to brag, to shove it in your faces that he took something from you."

Some*one*—not some*thing*. My eyes narrow, though I don't bother voicing the anger burning in my chest; Marcel's intentions are not malicious. Instead, I scratch the copper stubble along my jaw to hide how tightly it's clenched. I haven't bothered shaving in days, and it's starting to irritate my skin. "That doesn't explain the break in the connection," I point out in a gruff voice. "Unless she—"

"No," Marcel says over me, shaking his head. "Do you believe she's dead, Gabriel?"

My throat constricts, and I frown at the difficulty I find when trying to swallow. "No." I don't believe it—I refuse to.

"Right. Then there's another explanation we haven't considered yet. Blood oaths are tricky things. You guys knew that when you entered into it all those years ago." He flicks his wrist back and forth. "Witches and their spells."

My eyes widen as a thought hits me with the speed of a train. "A spell," I say. "Wherever Calla is could have a spell blocking our connection to her."

Marcel purses his lips. "It's possible."

Not only is it possible, it's a far better alternative than

what's got my stomach in painful knots. What has kept all of us up every night since she disappeared.

"I don't suppose you have a witch handy?"

"Wouldn't matter anyway, considering the only witch that could undo the block is the one who put it in place."

I slam my fist down on the armrest. "What am I supposed to do with that?" I growl without looking in Marcel's direction. I don't direct the question at him because I don't expect him to have an answer, though I really wish he did.

I scrub a hand down my face and sigh.

*Why did you have to run, angel?*

"I mean this with the utmost respect and only mention it out of concern for your wellbeing. You look like absolute shit. You're not going to be able to help Calla if you end up passing out from exhaustion or snapping and getting caught chowing down on a human because you're starving. You need to take care of yourself." His voice is stern but laced with worry.

I manage a weak smile. "Your concern is noted and appreciated."

"And ignored," he remarks dryly, shaking his head before he pins me with a level stare. "I'm serious, Gabriel. I don't know her much at all, but I can't see her wanting you—or the others for that matter—to get to a point where you're not giving yourself basic necessities because it could take away from potentially finding her. You're no good to her like this, okay? So smarten up."

My hands curl around the armrests, making the wood groan under my grip. He's right.

"Listen, I know you want to get back to Washington, but I think you should stay tonight. Take a break from everything and refocus. I know of a place that has voluntary feeders on standby. I'll text you the address. Go and replenish your strength." He nods, his voice stern but kind as he says, "Take care of yourself, Gabe."

I rise from the chair at the same moment Marcel stands, finding it in me to smile at him. "Thank you, Marcel. You know we appreciate the work you do for us, but you constantly go above and beyond to show how much you care. It doesn't go unnoticed, I hope you know that."

He shoots me a grin, and we walk through the main level, the aged hardwood creaking under our steps as we near the front door.

Marcel slaps me on the back as he opens the door for me. "Keep me posted. You know where I am if you need anything."

"Thank you," I tell him again, stepping out into the bitter afternoon air.

"Gabriel," Marcel calls, causing me to turn back. "You're going to find her."

I nod, jogging down the concrete steps in front of his townhouse to the sidewalk, where the wind picks up, the cold air making my cheeks tingle.

We *are* going to find her.

And then whoever is behind taking her from us will live to regret the decision… until we slaughter them.

❦  2  ❦

## CALLA

The pressure in my temples makes it hard to open my eyes. Painful even. Like jackhammers pounding into my head at every angle. I manage to pry them open slowly, immediately squinting at the lamp casting light across my face. Blinking hard in an attempt to clear the blur spattered across my vision, I turn away from the light, groaning as my muscles protest the sudden movement.

I have the fleeting thought that I'm dead, but I quickly dispel it. If I was dead, surely it wouldn't hurt so damn much.

When I attempt to sit up, I grit my teeth against the ache in my back. I haven't felt this awful since I got the flu in freshman year, and Brighton ended up having to take care of me as if I was a child.

*Brighton.*

Holy shit.

I'd been heading for her apartment when Dante grabbed me off the sidewalk. I needed to warn her, to tell her what I found in Atlas's office. She needs to know they're following her, that something in her family's company is connected to them.

My eyes go wide as they dart around the unfamiliar, dark bedroom. The haze in my head evaporates, replaced by panic, making my chest tighten as I press my shaking palm against the warmth of my skin over my heart.

Frowning, I peer down at the black silk slip I'm wearing, and my pulse races. My stomach twists into knots, making the possibility of puking on these lavish, no doubt expensive sheets very real.

Everything comes back at once, making my head spin and my eyes prick with hot tears. This overwhelming sense of dread is like nothing I've experienced before. Just when I thought I was starting to get a grip on all of this vampire blood oath shit, the rug has been pulled out from under me.

All the secrets, Atlas being involved in Ellis Industries, the creepy surveillance photos of Brighton... Then being ambushed outside of her apartment by Dante.

My heart beats hard against my chest as the memories flood in. The fear that overtook me when I realized Dante had found me. The indescribable pain I felt when he sank his fangs into my neck.

I suck in a shallow breath and lift my fingers to the spot he bit me, and when they graze smooth skin, I press my lips together. It's... healed. Which means one of two things— someone used vampire blood to heal me, or I've been here long enough for it to heal on its own. The former makes my stomach roil, but the latter makes me just as nauseous with panic.

Squeezing my eyes shut at the tingling sensation along my neck, I can't stop the scene from playing out in my head. The flash of his fangs, the sickening feeling of him drawing the blood out of me, and the woman killing him right in front of me. The memory of the sound of his heart thumping against the floor makes bile rise in my throat, and I swallow hard, unable to open my eyes as I relive the fuzzy moments after Dante was killed. The angelically attractive vampire cleaning the blood from her hand as if it was nothing but a mere inconvenience to her.

I press my fingers against the thrumming of pain in my temples. My shallow breathing quickens as I recall the woman's words.

*"Dante's ill-mannered, silly little excuse for revenge is not the reason you were brought here."*

What the hell am I doing here? And who is the vampire behind it?

Once I've managed to pull myself into a sitting position, I let out a breath and slowly swing my legs over the side of the bed. I take my time trying to stand, worried I'll fall over the second I'm upright. Sure enough, when I stand, the world tilts around me, and it takes a long moment to regain my balance. My head is light and fuzzy, as if I haven't eaten or drank any water in days. I've never felt this weak. I keep my eyes trained on the massive window in front of me. It's dark outside, but that could mean anything. It's possible I've been here for hours or days. There's no way to tell. I've been here long enough for someone to dress me. Shuddering at the thought, I take a tentative step toward the window. My legs are a little shaky as if I'd run a long distance without warming up, but they're sturdy enough for me to make it to the window. I press my hands against the cold glass, peering down to the street below. I have to be at least twenty stories up, possibly higher. *Too high to jump.* The sidewalk is empty and the street is mostly quiet, save for a couple of cars, their headlights casting a faint glow on the asphalt.

I turn back to the room and lean against the windowsill, watching the flickering flames in the massive black marble fireplace against the wall farthest from me. My head is full of questions, and not knowing if I'll be alive long enough to get the answers makes my breath catch in my throat.

My thoughts quickly go to the guys. For some reason, they must not know where I am, otherwise they'd be here. They would have come for me by now. Atlas would be lecturing me about leaving the house with Dante on the loose, Lex would be ready to kill whoever's behind this whole thing, Kade would be making inappropriate and mostly unhelpful commentary, and Gabriel... he would just want to make sure I was okay. As conflicted as part of me still feels about them, I wish they were here.

I shake my head. I can't think about my confusing emotions toward the vampires who claimed me right now. I need to figure out what the hell is going on here. That woman... Who the hell is she? And what could she possibly want me for? If she was going to kill me, she's had plenty of opportunities, so there has to be another reason. And honestly, that scares me more than her wanting me dead. Because death is easy. Whatever this is... I'm terrified to find out.

Making my way around the dim room, my eyes adjust to the warm light coming from the lamp next to the four-poster bed I'd been sleeping in. Everything about the space is elegant. Dark wood accents and deep, rich reds and browns. The large crimson afghan rug beneath my bare feet is plush, with an intricate design woven through it.

I find myself standing in front of a closed dark wood door. My hand hovers over the knob, fingers shaking.

Before I can push myself to wrap my fingers around the brass and turn it, the door opens from the other side, and I stumble back, my heart slamming against my ribcage.

I squint hard until the vampire in front of me comes into focus, looking as stunningly elegant as she had in the moments before she—

"You're awake," she says in a smooth voice, the corners of her lips curved slightly upward. "Good."

How long was I asleep?

How long have I been here?

These are the questions I should be asking. Instead, my legs shift back on their own, moving me away from the woman as she watches me with a curious glint in her bright silver eyes. After stepping into the room, leaving the door open, she clasps her hands behind her back. The way she exudes ease and power in equal measure has my heart beating like the wings of a hummingbird. I don't want to be afraid; I shouldn't show this vampire the fear that sings in my veins, but the weakness in my body makes it difficult to keep up my bravado. She can likely see right through it.

"Who are you?" I finally ask once I'm sure my voice won't waver or crack.

She flashes a brilliant, snow-white smile. Her teeth look too perfect, too straight and white to be real. Veneers, I'd guess. "My name is Selene. I apologize, I should have introduced myself the other night."

*The other night?*

Selene's eyes trail over me, and I fight the urge to look away. Her scrutiny is a heavy weight that makes my skin tingle uncomfortably. Probably because I know she can snuff me out with a simple flick of her wrist if she wants. She's no longer wearing the flowing white dress, which confirms my suspicion that some time has passed since I was brought here. Instead, she's wearing a tight-fitting plum dress with a sharp V-shaped neckline and a hem that just barely reaches her knees, plus some seriously impressive heels. She towers over me, which really doesn't help how intimidated I am by her.

She tilts her head to the side ever so slightly. "You and I have much to discuss, Calla."

My chest tightens. I have no idea who this woman is, so the idea of having anything to talk about doesn't make much sense to me. But if a conversation with her is going to give me the answer to why I'm here—as much as I'm dreading finding out—I should just get it over with. "I—"

"Perhaps we can chat once you've had a chance to clean yourself up and have something to eat."

As much as I desperately want and need both of those things, I cross my arms over my chest, trying to appear more confident than I feel in this scrap of black lace and silk in front of a stranger who is most likely over a century older than me and, you know, supernatural. "I think we should talk now."

The vampire arches a perfectly shaped brow. "You can barely stand upright but you wish to refuse my offer in order to keep some semblance of control? Very well." Selene walks across the room at an unhurried pace, her strides confident and graceful. She lowers herself into one of the red velvet wingback chairs in front of the fireplace, crossing one leg over the other and resting her hands in her lap. She stares at the flames crackling in front of her, and a small smile touches her rose-colored lips. "What is it you'd like to know, Calla?"

I stare at Selene for a few seconds, finding myself wondering why she lit the fireplace in this room she's keeping me in. I find it hard to believe it's for my comfort, considering she knocked me out cold when we met. Is she trying to trick me into trusting her? Hesitantly, I make my way to the chair across from her. Lowering myself into it, the silk glides easily along the velvet. I grip the armrests, too tight at first, before I remember I'm trying to appear less freaked out than I currently am. I force my fingers to relax as my eyes flick between Selene and the light emanating from the fireplace. "I have a lot of questions," I start, dragging my gaze back to her. "How long have I been here?" I ask first.

She tips her head to the side. "A few days, give or take."

"Three or four?" I press, my pulse kicking up.

Arching a brow, her tone is mocking when she asks, "That's your main concern? What, do you have somewhere else to be, Calla?"

*Um, yeah. Literally anywhere else.* I want to say it, but I'm so out of my element here, I bite my tongue and keep my mouth shut.

Selene rolls her eyes. "Relax. There can't be anything that important in your mundane life you could've missed in the last week. You've been fed and taken care of until I was ready to have this conversation with you. I even healed Dante's little..." She points toward my neck, and I shudder at her confirmation that I'd been fed vampire blood.

A million follow up questions race around my head. I don't remember anything from the last week that I've been here, which likely means she's been glamouring me. Despite the swirling urge in my stomach to purge whatever food she's forced me to eat, I need to know why I'm here. "You said..." My voice trails off as the memory from the night I was brought here threatens to replay in my head. I clear my throat and try again. "You said Dante wasn't the reason I was brought here, so I'm left to wonder, to assume, the reason is you."

Selene nods, tapping her fingers against her knee as she regards me thoughtfully. She offers a ghost of a smile that does nothing to ease the knots in my stomach. "Yes, well, I had to get a look at you for myself."

Shaking my head, I ask, "Why? Why do you care about me at all?"

Her eyes take on a light of amusement. "*Care* is a strong word. Call it a mild fascination."

I frown. "That still doesn't answer my question."

"Why," she echoes, pursing her lips for a moment. "We have a mutual friend, you and I."

*A mutual friend.*

My back stiffens against the chair, and I sit up straighter. The only possibility would be one of the guys.

Selene nods. "You're putting it together," she observes.

"I'm really not," I disagree. "You know about the blood oath, that I can guess, but that doesn't explain why you had me grabbed off the street."

"Those boys of yours kept you locked up tight for a while," she muses, glancing toward the flames. The light dances across her flawless complexion as she continues, "I'll admit, I was a little surprised when Dante reached out and let me know you were with him. I truly didn't think he'd manage to get to you, not with those vampires' determination to keep you safe."

"*Safe* is a strong word," I echo her previous sentiment without thinking.

She laughs, a soft, melodic sound that floats through the air and makes my cheeks heat. "You're alive, aren't you?"

"I'm a prisoner—again," I point out. "The secrets continue to pile up, and I'm left with more questions than answers."

"Allow me to answer one then. You're wondering which of those gorgeous vampires you've been bound to is tied to me."

I nod, because I really can't figure it out. I can't see it being Atlas; in a way, the two seem too alike. Lex, I think, would be too eccentric, and Kade... well, maybe Kade. He's been known to surprise me on occasion. Or Gabriel. I wholeheartedly believe he could be friends with anyone. Despite what brought us together, I have no doubt that Gabriel's heart is good. He's kind and compassionate, and fuck, I *miss* him.

"Gabriel and I go way back," Selene reveals, leaning against the back of the chair as she lifts a hand to her long white-blond hair, fingering one of the curls and smiling to herself as if she's reliving a fond memory of the two of them.

It twists something in my gut, and I clench my jaw, wanting to look away. Instead, I ask, "How do you know Gabriel?"

Her eyes meet mine, and her next words make the blood in my veins turn to ice.

"I'm the one who turned him."

## 3

## GABRIEL

New York City is one of my favorite places in the United States, but walking down the sidewalk with brownstones on either side of the car-lined street brings me little joy when the only thing on my mind is the fiery human I'm finding it alarmingly difficult to be apart from.

I'm heading toward the subway station when my phone buzzes in the pocket of my black windbreaker. I pull it out in a flash, hoping for an update from Washington, but my stomach sinks when I realize that isn't what it is. Instead, I'm looking at a message from Fallon, one of the vampires I met during my stint living in Manhattan almost forty years ago.

*Heard you were around. Jase and I are heading out for drinks. Let's meet.*

I stop walking and move out of the way of foot traffic.

*Hey, Fal. I'm not in the city long. Maybe next time?*

Her response comes less than a minute later. *Don't make me drag your ass out. I'm sending you the address of this new place we found last week. It's super casual, so you'd better not be in a suit. See you in an hour!*

I sigh into the air, fogging it with my breath. It's unseasonably chilly for April, and I've never been one to enjoy the cold. *Fine*, I type back, *but I can't stay long.*

She sends back an eye-roll emoji, then adds, *Looking forward to seeing you too, Gabe.*

As much as the Manhattan social scene isn't something I'm in the mood for right now, this could be a good opportunity to catch up with Fallon and Jase and see if they've heard anything about Dante or the hunters in the tristate area. Marcel does an excellent job keeping his ear to the ground, but it's always good to keep tabs elsewhere. Finding Calla is the priority, but unfortunately, we can't forget about the ever-growing organization of people whose goal is to eradicate our kind.

☙❦❧

The place Marcel sent me to is essentially a glamorous feeder den. From the pristine white brick exterior, it looks like a private, luxury spa, but the mouth-watering scent of blood overwhelms my senses the moment I round the corner and before I even spot the building.

Stepping inside, I'm immediately enveloped in warmth. I'm glad to be out of the cold, but the atmosphere here has unease coiling in my stomach. It isn't my first time in a place like this—not by far. I spent the first full year after I turned in a haze of bloodlust and feeder dens, though most of those places weren't nearly as nice as this.

The space smells of sandalwood and citrus mixed with some kind of oil—a heady herbal aroma that does little to ease the ache in my temples.

I walk further into the bright, patron-free room, my shoes silent on the polished dark wood floor. The décor is simple yet warm, welcoming. To one side is a set of gray plush couches around a glass coffee table with lit candles flickering atop it, and to the other is—

A soft gasp from behind the white and gold marble reception desk snags my attention, and I glance at the pale, black-haired girl who is staring at me with wide, olive-green eyes.

Sometimes I forget how well-known we are among the vampires. Though this girl—who can't be older than twenty—is entirely human. The wall behind her is made of light-colored rocks and has a water feature built in. It's meant to be relaxing, I'm sure, but the trickling sound is grinding on my nerves. I'm more on edge than normal—a quick feeding should take care of that, at least a bit. I won't be myself again until we have Calla back, but until then, Marcel is right. I need to take care of my basic necessities.

"H-hi," the girl stammers, a blush tingeing her cheeks pink as she pushes the dark-rimmed glasses up the bridge of her nose. "Mr. Simmons, it's such an honor to have you visit our facility."

I offer a polite smile. I'm not in the mood for pleasantries, but this girl doesn't deserve to be exposed to the wrath living just below the surface. My jaw clenches as my gaze flicks to the vein in her neck, pulsing with the rampant beat of her heart. I swallow hard, struggling to ignore the pressure building in my gums.

"Thank you," I force out, dropping my gaze to the shiny metal name tag attached to her white blouse, "Emerson."

Her blush deepens, and she quickly turns her attention to the tablet in her hand. "If you'd like to follow me, we have a VIP room ready for you." She steps out from behind the counter and opens a set of frosted glass doors, her heels clicking softly on the wood floor that seems to carry throughout the place.

I follow her down a hallway with closed doors lining both sides. The air is filled with essential oils and warmth, but through that, I pick up on the sharp, metallic scent. The reason I'm here—blood.

"Marcel let me know you might be coming by," Emerson says, stealing a glance at me over her shoulder as we continue toward the end of the hall to another set of glass doors. "We don't always have, um, staff on-site for the… treatment you'll be getting, but I was able to call someone in."

I nod as soft piano music plays overhead, seemingly from a speaker in the ceiling, though I can't see it through the collection of chandeliers that line the hallway.

We stop in front of the doors, and I say, "It's much appreciated."

"No problem at all." She pulls out a badge and taps it against a panel in the wall. It gives a soft *beep* and a lock clicks. Emerson opens the door, and I grab it, holding it for her to walk ahead. "Thank you," she says, blushing again.

My lips twitch. If this girl knew how old I was… Though perhaps she's intrigued by it. Not many humans know of our kind, but of the ones who do—even though they're mostly glamoured—can't help but be curious. Some even want to be turned. This isn't a life I would wish on anyone, but it's hard to deter someone who desperately desires eternity.

She walks into the room, the lights turning on automatically. It's a small, inviting space, set up like a living room with the same dark floors from the rest of the building and pale gray walls. Emerson walks toward the plush couch against the wall across the room and straightens one of the black throw pillows.

"Make yourself comfortable, and I will send Jackie in right away."

I shrug off my jacket, hanging it on one of the hooks next to the door. "Excellent," I say, meeting her gaze. "Thank you for your assistance."

She catches her lip between her teeth and nods, her pulse

ticking unevenly, then offers a wide smile. "Oh, of course! Please let me know if there's anything else I can do to make your visit more pleasant."

Nodding, my lips curl into a hint of a smile as I turn away from her, walking toward the sitting area. The air is filled with the faint scent of lavender and vanilla, and my shoes make barely any sound on the soft beige area rug on the floor.

The door clicks shut as I lower myself onto the couch and let out a slow breath. This place is a little much for me, but coming recommended by Marcel, I know it's good. Plus, I need to feed. It may as well be from a willing human who is being compensated for her... donation instead of some unsuspecting human off the street. The act of feeding was something I used to enjoy. I relished in the feeling of over-taking my prey, bending them to my will, and taking their life force to make myself stronger.

A shudder ripples through me, and I blink hard. That was a very long time ago. I was a different person then, under the thumb of the monster who created me. She was also the first woman I ever loved.

I growl low in my throat, shoving away those thoughts and clenching my jaw before I realize a small red-headed woman has slipped into the room.

Her wide brown eyes flit around, and she stammers, "I'm sorry. Should I come back?"

"No." I force my expression to soften. "Please come in. I apologize. It's been..." I stop myself, then repeat, "Please come in."

She closes the door and approaches slowly. I see the hesitation in her gaze and the uneven beat of her heart. She's wearing light gray scrubs as if she's about to give me a massage.

I shift closer to the edge of the couch, resting my hands

casually in my lap. "Have you done this before?" I ask, attempting to put the young woman, Jackie, I recall the receptionist mentioning, at ease. It's been too long since I fed, and all I want to do is tear into her throat, but I can control myself. I can make this experience enjoyable for her.

The tension in her shoulders fades a little, and she smiles. "Oh, yes. I've been in the service of vampires for many years."

That has my brows lifting. She doesn't look much older than Emerson. "How many years?" I ask as she walks around the glass coffee table in front of the couch and sits next to me, angling her body toward mine.

"You think I'm too young," she says with a smile. Her pulse has returned to a normal pace; she's becoming more relaxed around me.

I lean against the back of the couch, resting my arm along it as I turn to face her as well. "How old *are* you?"

She purses her lips. "How old are *you*?"

A surprised laugh escapes me. "Ah, come on. I asked you first."

It's her turn to laugh. "Really? That's what you're going with?"

I shrug. "Guess."

"Based on your comeback, I'd say you can't be much older than twenty-five." Her voice takes on a flirtatious tone, and the predator in me latches on to it before I can stop myself. I might have the self-control to keep myself from killing her, but playing into this game we've started is another story.

"Hmm. Take that and multiply it by five and you'll be a little closer." I shift toward her, snaring her gaze. Her breath hitches before I say, "Your turn."

Her eyes stay locked on mine. "I'm twenty-seven." She collects the hair from her neck, pulling it over her shoulder. "But people have always thought I was younger." She shrugs. "Must have something to do with my genes. Anyway..." She moves closer and turns her head, exposing her throat. "Whenever you're ready."

The moment my eyes land on the pulse in her neck, my fangs spring forward and my throat burns so intensely, I'm reaching for her, sliding my arm around her narrow waist and pulling her closer in a matter of seconds. My nose grazes her neck first, making her shiver against me, and I inhale before sinking my fangs into her carotid artery. Blood flows into my mouth, the hot, metallic taste exploding on my tongue. My eyes close, and I drink deeply, warmth trickling through me as I regain my strength. Her heartbeat slows, and she leans into me more, but I don't stop. She moans, and the sound goes right to my cock.

My eyes fly open, and I pull away from her, standing and wiping my mouth with the back of my hand. I've had more than enough for now, anyway.

She slumps against the back of the couch, her eyelids fluttering as blood runs down the side of her neck. Shit. I should have healed the bite marks. Too late. I'm already backing toward the door, grabbing my jacket and shrugging it on. I reach for the door handle, but stop myself, letting out a ragged breath before walking back to the couch. I pull Jackie forward and drag my tongue along the small puncture marks, sealing them. When I pull back, her eyes are still closed and her lips are curved into a content smile. She's been at this a while, which likely means she's addicted to this feeling. The headiness, the feeling of floating… I remember it all too well.

I lift my hand to her face, tucking a bit of her hair behind her ear. "Take care," I murmur before heading for the door again. This time, I don't hesitate. I leave the room, closing the door behind me.

Luckily, Emerson isn't at the desk when I walk through

the reception area, so I slip back outside without further interaction with her.

My strides are hurried. I'm not sure where I'm going, but I need to keep moving. I haven't been that affected by a feed in a long time. On the precipice of losing control—and being aroused by it. I could have done anything to that girl, and she would have let me—my venom would've made her think she *wanted* it, even if she truly didn't.

I pick up my pace, weaving through people on the sidewalk. If the street weren't so busy, I would have used my vampire speed to get the hell out of here by now.

Trying to blend in among the humans can really be a pain in the ass sometimes.

"I can see by the look on your face that wasn't the answer you were expecting." Selene's voice is laced with amusement as she leans back, keeping her eyes on me.

I stare at her, unable to make my lips move to form a word let alone a sentence to respond. This woman turned Gabriel into a vampire. Even the guys don't know about how Gabriel came into his immortality—Lex had told me that much the night I went with him to the tattoo shop—and I'm sitting across from her.

"No," I finally say, quickly licking my lips to combat the dryness.

She nods. "I turned Gabriel, siring him to me for the duration of our immortal lives. Mind you, our connection runs far deeper than the silly little blood oath you've wound up in."

Is... is she *bragging?*

I'm so fucking confused.

"H-how long ago was that?" I ask.

She presses a shiny, manicured finger to her lips in thought. "Hmm... It's hard to say. Time is a little different once you become a vampire, Calla. Years and decades are mere blips of time when you live forever. Surely you've considered that by now."

The knots in my stomach tighten. "Considered living forever? Not really. I'm just trying to make it to graduation." School is the least of my concerns considering my current situation, but still.

Her lips twitch. "You *are* a naive one, aren't you?"

"Why am I here?" I blurt, shifting in the chair and glancing around. "Where is *here*, anyway? Clearly you have some way of blocking the connection between me and them, otherwise they would have come for me by now, and you would be dead."

I have to believe that. If they knew where I was, they would be here. There has to be a reason—something that is keeping them away. The only vulnerability I'm aware of is white ash, though I don't know if it can be used to block a vampire's tracking capability. If so, maybe this place has it in the walls, making it impossible for them to find me. That would mean their adversity to white ash is stronger than their connection to my blood. But I truly have no idea. I can barely think straight at this point.

The hint of a smile fades from Selene's lips, though her tone is still light. "Is that right?"

Fear and anger go to war in my chest, kicking up my pulse as the fire crackles in the fireplace next to me, making my cheeks and chest flushed. "Why am I here?" I ask again.

"I was curious about you," she says simply, as if the reasoning behind my kidnapping should be obvious. "You're involved in Gabriel's life, so naturally, it was important for us to meet." She smooths her hands down the front of her dress, not that there was a single wrinkle in it to begin with. Selene seems like the type to have her clothes dry cleaned and steamed prior to wearing. "I had a friend of mine put a protective barrier around my property to ensure the two of us wouldn't be interrupted by your entourage of vampires."

My brows tug together, and I choose to skip over the whole *protective barrier* thing. I don't think I have the mental capacity to dive into *that* right now. "You don't get a piece of me just because he does and you're his sire or whatever." I shake my head and add dryly, "This isn't a pyramid scheme."

When she smiles at me this time, I get a flash of her fangs. "Perhaps not, but I am prepared to offer you a deal. One I think you'll be very interested in hearing."

"What are you talking about?" I pick at the skin around my thumbnail, avoiding her sharp silver eyes. The weight in my gut tells me I'm not ready to hear what she's offering, but I don't see that I have much of a choice.

"Don't worry," she says in a smooth voice, "this is very simple and straightforward."

I force myself to meet her gaze. "What do you want?"

Selene's lips curl into a slow smile. "I want Gabriel."

My stomach plummets, and I feel as if my ribcage is closing in tighter by the second. I clench my jaw, fighting the urge to snap at Selene, despite knowing full well I wouldn't stand a chance against her. I wasn't expecting to feel so... possessive over Gabriel. But the thought of this woman getting her claws in him makes me want to scream.

"What does that have to do with me?" I ask in a strained voice. I need to tread lightly, choose my words carefully. If her response to Dante is any indication, this woman doesn't give a shit about others' lives.

"Gabriel cares very deeply for you." Her tone makes it clear she isn't sure why. "If anyone can help me get him back, I would imagine you'd be the one."

"Get him back," I echo, desperately trying to find my way through her web of history with Gabriel. "What... what happened after you turned him?" There's a reason they aren't together anymore, and considering whatever it is wasn't something he would tell the guys he sees as brothers, it has to be pretty twisted. And she wants me to help send him back to her.

"That's ancient history. What matters now is us finding our way back to each other."

"Is this the part where you tell me you love him?" I ask, an edge to my voice.

Gabriel made it very clear from the night we met that I belonged to him and the others. That shit is a two-way street, and I'm not about to let this vampire screw with that. Yeah, I'm pissed as hell at all the guys for keeping me in the dark for so long, and they're going to hear about it plenty once we're together. But this woman trying to lay claim to Gabriel has my hackles standing straight.

"Something like that," she muses, continuing to twirl a curl around her finger as her eyes flick between mine. "You see, having a sire means many things. One of which is that when Gabriel is close it makes me stronger. Especially when I'm drinking his blood."

*Vampires feed on other vampires?*

"So you want him because he can give you more power?" I ask, my stomach twisting painfully. Selene doesn't care about Gabriel, not really—she cares about what he can do for her.

Those silver eyes narrow at me. "Before you refuse," she says in a smooth voice, "don't you wish to know what I could give you in return?"

I shake my head automatically. Whatever she could offer would never be enough for me to trick Gabriel into returning to this... this monster. I can't help the flare of protectiveness rippling through me. This whole thing would be so much easier if I didn't care about the vampires who tore into my life over a month ago and ripped everything apart. Damn them for making me give a shit.

"Hmm." A sly grin spreads across her lips, making my breath hitch. "Not even if I told you I have the power to break the blood oath you're trapped in? To free you from the vampires' claim to you? Think about it, Calla. You could have your life back, could have a future that *you* choose."

I grit my teeth, willing the sudden burn of tears back. *Do not cry in front of this bitch.* Before I can stop myself, I ask, "How would that even work?"

Selene slides her hands along the armrests on either side of her, flicking her tongue along her bottom lip. "As you can imagine, I've been around a long time. I've curated certain relationships with very powerful people in my world. Over the decades, I've grown quite close with the York clan. Now, you may not know just how important a vampire Atlas is, but the Yorks are infamous—practically royalty in the vampire world."

My eyes go wide. "I don't... What does that have to do with the blood oath?"

She grants me a polite, albeit strained smile. "What are the terms of your vow to them, Calla?"

"Um, I'm basically stuck with them until I die."

She curls her fingers over the edge of the chair, her nail polish shining in the firelight. "Or?"

I blink at her, and then it hits me. "Or until they allow me to sever the contract. But that's—"

"Never going to happen?" she offers. "Why don't you leave that up to me?"

"What are you going to do?" I curse inwardly at my words; it sounds as if I've already accepted her offer.

"Atlas's parents owe me a favor from many, many years ago. I think it's time I collect." The corner of her mouth lifts into an amused smile. "And the others will follow him.

Gabriel, maybe not, but that won't be a problem. I'll force his hand if I must."

"You can do that?" I ask in a quiet voice, my pulse kicking up.

She chuckles. "I can glamour Gabriel as easily as I can glamour you."

I shake my head. "Then why haven't you?"

The glimmer in her eyes remains. "Where's the fun in that? I'll get what I want in the end, but that doesn't mean it has to be quick or boringly easy. I enjoy a challenge."

I grit my teeth against the bile rising in my throat at her words. My thoughts are spinning, going a million miles a minute as I try to wrap my mind around all of this. "You would do all of this just to get Gabriel back? Even if he wants nothing to do with you? Is the power really worth it?"

Selene inhales and exhales slowly, regarding me with a smooth expression. "Our world is changing," she says in a deeper tone, "and only those strong enough to stand against their enemies will make it out alive."

"So all of this is just about power," I say, "You couldn't care less about Gabriel." The twist of jealousy I felt earlier quickly morphs into anger. I don't want this woman anywhere near Gabriel.

She inclines her head slightly. "Just," she echoes with a laugh. "You underestimate the importance of that power, Calla. But of course you do. You know nothing about the world you've been forced into." She offers me a thoughtful glance. "So allow me to help free you of it."

I want to open my mouth and tell her to go to hell. That I'd never consider what she's offering even for a second. But I'd be lying. I have no idea how she expects me to get Gabriel to return to her—not to mention, the thought of doing that makes me want to keel over and vomit the noth-ingness in my stomach. Try as I might, I can't deny that the idea of being in control of my future is enticing. Dangerously so.

"Why now?" I ask.

She exhales slowly, as if I'm testing her patience. "The threat against our kind continues to grow stronger every day. I'm doing what I must to ensure my own survival." A cruel, suggestive smile paints her lips. "Plus, you've been with Gabriel, haven't you?" She doesn't wait for me to answer before she rises from her chair. "Take your time and consider what I've offered you, Calla." She walks toward the door without turning back, but she does add, "In the meantime, you need to eat and regain some strength. I'll have the house-keeper bring something up shortly."

The door clicks shut behind her, and a shiver crawls through me despite the warmth emanating from the fire-place. Alone with nothing but the soft crackle of flames next to me, my mind takes a dive back to being brought here. I try desperately to think through each minute, everything that happened from being grabbed off the street, all the way to the moment everything went dark. Bile rises in my throat at the horrific, blood-chilling memory of Dante's unforgiving grip on me. The way he taunted me before sinking his teeth into my throat and drinking my blood.

I swallow hard, shaking my head in an attempt to shove the memory of sharp pain away. It's not one that will soon fade. That's if it ever does.

As much as I've wanted to escape my fate of being tied to the vampires, the idea of selling Gabriel out, forcing him to return to his sire makes my stomach roil. Of all people, he doesn't deserve that.

Blinking back the sudden onslaught of tears, I press my fist to my lips, struggling to hold back the sound.

I can't do it.

It isn't me... and I don't want to be the type of person that would cause another pain for the purpose of their own gain. The way Gabriel came into my life doesn't matter, not in this sense.

As much as I want my life back—and the idea of freedom and a real future, one that *I* choose—I can't destroy someone else's life to achieve that.

I still don't trust the guys, and I haven't a clue what Brighton's family is involved in that links them to the vampires I'm bound to, but I am hellbent on figuring it out.

Which pretty much leaves me with only one option: I need to figure out a way to get the hell away from here. Preferably alive.

## 5

## GABRIEL

I arrive at the address Fallon sent and find what appears to be a small dive bar. Getting out of the town car, I step onto the sidewalk and shut the door. The music inside isn't blaring, but it's loud enough to hear when the old, stained glass door opens ahead of me as a group of patrons with whiskey on their breath leave the green brick building.

I walk inside when the doorway is clear, and the sound of Fallon's excited squeal catches my attention immediately. I turn toward it and have less than a second to prepare myself for her to throw her arms around my neck, hugging me as if I'd just returned from war. It *has* been a while since I visited.

The floral scent of her perfume overwhelms me as I wrap my arms around her narrow waist and hug her tightly, pressing a chaste kiss to her cheek when she pulls back. "Fallon," I greet with an easy smile. "Long time no see."

She punches my arm. "Yeah, no kidding. Jerk."

Jase approaches from behind her, shaking his head and grinning at me, flashing a bit of fang. "Long time indeed. You look like shit."

"You know, people keep telling me that," I mutter as the

two lead me to the booth they secured near the back of the room. The bar is crowded with mostly middle-aged people. This place certainly isn't a popular hangout spot for the students in the city. Most of the people here are at least fifty years old.

I slide into the booth, glancing around the dark space. The walls are wood panels, covered in curling and ripped rock band posters. The scent of smoke and liquor hangs heavy in the air, and though I don't see anyone actively smoking, nicotine clings to their clothes.

"What brings you to the city?" Jase asks.

I turn my attention back to my friends as they sip on their beers, waiting for me to answer. "It's sort of a long story."

"Such a shame we aren't immortal," Fallon remarks dryly with a mocking sigh, sticking her tongue out at me when I roll my eyes. She ties her bright red corkscrew curls back and dumps a handful of peanuts into her mouth. The black tank top she's wearing is barely containing her breasts, much to the delight of the men at the bar. Not that she notices.

"Something's wrong," Jase says, his voice serious as he looks at me.

I press my lips together for a moment, debating how I should start. "We fulfilled the blood oath."

He shoves a hand through his obsidian-colored hair. "Shit, bro. When did that happen?"

"A month ago."

He nods. "How did it go?"

I exhale on a laugh. "About as well as we expected. Calla knew about the deal her family made with us, but she didn't know when we were coming. She was pretty pissed."

Fallon arches a brow. "I mean, fair enough, Gabe. I'd be pissed too, and I actually like you. The others mind you…"

I just shake my head at her. She and Kade had a fling a few decades ago that ended with her burning his favorite jacket. I never asked, and neither brought it up. "Anyway, we were trying to keep her away from all of the hunter shit we're dealing with, but as you can imagine, after having her future dictated by an ancestor before she was born, and her life now controlled by the vampires she was bound to, she wasn't much of a fan of being kept in the dark."

"Can you blame her?" Jase asks, setting his pint down on the wooden table. There's sticky residue covering it, as if they don't clean them very well—or at all.

"Of course not. And when Dante started sniffing around for her, we had to tell her about him. Well, some of it. She knows he was involved with the business her family was in here and that he was seeking revenge against her for what went down."

Fallon scoffs. "He went after that poor girl because he got screwed out of some money."

"Some money," Jase echoes, downing the rest of his drink. "Last time I checked, twenty million dollars isn't just *some money*, my love."

She rolls her eyes. "Whatever. That shit has nothing to do with—what's her name again?"

"Calla," I say. Her name on my lips makes my chest tighten.

Fallon nods. "So what's going on now?"

My jaw clenches. "She's gone."

Her eyes widen. "Gone. What do you mean gone? I thought the blood oath connected you to her?"

"Something's blocking it. Marcel thinks it's a barrier spell."

"Fucking witches," Jase mutters under his breath.

Vampires and witches have never gotten along very well. Centuries of bad blood between the species has gone unresolved. It's not something I intend to add to my list of problems, but if I found out a witch helped keep Calla from us...

"So what, you think Dante took her?"

I rehash the conversation I had with Marcel, and they agree that Dante's insufferable personality would make it near impossible for him to go without bragging about his conquest if he'd been the one to take Calla.

"You two haven't heard anything from him lately?" I check, just to make sure.

"Nah," Fallon says, tracing her finger along the rim of her glass. She stops, flicking her gaze to mine. "Nothing about Dante, and I'm not sure this is really something you ought to be worrying about right now on top of everything else, but I did hear of Selene showing up around Greenwich a month or so ago. Before that, she hadn't been in the city for years that I know of."

"She was sniffing around looking for you," Jase adds. "When she found out you were living in Washington with your friends, she left New York pretty fast."

My hands clench into fists as a shiver rips through me at the mention of my sire. The sounds of the room around us— the glasses clinking and people talking over the rock music playing—fade in and out as my chest constricts, making my pulse race.

Selene could have used our sire connection to find me once she got to Washington, though trying to track me from New York may not have worked. Distance, from what I've learned, can make tracking through the sire connection difficult.

Sweat dots my brow and upper lip as my eyes bounce between my friends. They know very little about the woman who turned me and the relationship I had with her, which is how it will remain. Not even my brothers know of the horror that was the first year of my life as a vampire. My memories are filled with bloodshed, thoughtless killing, and depraved sex with the monster I believed I loved. Who I naively thought loved me in return, which was her reason for gifting me eternal life.

How wrong I'd been.

Selene wanted nothing but power. Control. Over me and the other vampires she turned. She would never admit to building an army, but that's exactly what we were. She sired us to stay with her, made us believe we were some kind of family.

It took me a long time to figure out that we were being manipulated. By then, I'd killed so many people... I could never forgive myself for the monster I'd become. I did the only thing I could do—I left her.

That was over a century ago, but to this day, I can't get rid of the dark, sickening feel of her claws dug into my chest, my very soul.

Ice shoots through my veins and my back stiffens against the plastic booth. I can't explain the sensations racing through me; I have to get out of here. I need to get home.

"Gabriel—"

My voice shakes as I force out, "It's her."

Jase's dark brows pull together. "What are you talking about, Gabe?"

"She took her," I say through gritted teeth. My gums throb as my fangs threaten to extend and cut through them.

Fallon sucks in a breath, frowning at me from across the table. "You think Selene has Calla?"

I shake my head, a low growl rumbling through my chest. "I *know* she does."

My friends exchange a wary glance as I get out of the booth and head for the door without saying goodbye. Son of a bitch—I should have figured it out sooner. Anger rips through me like a vicious wave, and I fight the urge to put my fist through one of the brick exteriors I pass along the sidewalk.

I pull my phone out of my pocket as I hail a cab, not having enough time to wait for my town car. Getting in the back, I bark at the driver to head to the airstrip I flew into a couple of days ago. He pulls away from the curb with a silent nod, and I don't bother buckling my seatbelt as I scroll through my contacts and select Atlas's name.

"Gabriel." Atlas's voice is low, tired. We're all exhausted, barely sleeping these days. Every waking hour is important; *we have to find her.*

"I know who has her."

There's a beat of silence on the other end, and then, "Who?"

I close my eyes, struggling to focus on Atlas instead of the growing pressure in my chest. "The woman who turned me," I say through gritted teeth, low enough the driver can't over-hear my words.

"Why the fuck would your sire take Calla?"

My grip on the phone tightens, threatening to snap the thing in half if I'm not careful. I let out a slow breath, finally prying my eyes open. "It's a long story. Not one I can get into right now." I glance out the window as we fly down the free-way. "I'm getting on a plane shortly. I'll be home soon and then I will explain everything." My voice starts to shake with unbridled anger. The story of my turning was never one I wanted to relive—and certainly not one I wanted to share with the guys. But I'm left with no choice. They need to know—Calla's life depends on it.

"Lex will meet you at the airport. Whatever this is, Gabriel, we're going to figure it out."

I end the call without another word, glaring at my phone screen for several moments that feel like their own eternities.

Then, with a shaky hand, I dial a number I regrettably know by heart and lift the phone to my ear, my pulse pounding in my throat. I can't say how I know for certain—

perhaps it's the familiar weight on my chest and tingling in my veins, or maybe it's intuition. Because Marcel was right. If Dante took her, we'd know it by now, mostly due to his need to brag. No one else would have the guts to make a move against us like this. It… it has to be her.

Each ring feels longer than the last. My heart beats in my throat, and my stomach plummets when the call is answered.

"I was wondering how long it was going to take you to put it together."

My entire body goes rigid at the soft, melodic sound of her voice. I haven't heard it in years, and still, I respond to it automatically. Memories flash in front of my eyes; nights of drinking until we were drunk—on alcohol and blood. Fucking in different clubs around the world, surrounded by vampires and humans alike, but all I saw was red. And her. Always her.

It was a lifetime ago.

"What have you done with her?" I ground out.

Selene chuckles, and the sound presses into my chest, making it harder to breathe. "That's the first thing you want to say to me? After so long?" She tuts her tongue. "I have to say, I'm disappointed."

"I don't care," I snap. "Where is Calla?"

"Your little human is perfectly safe. In fact, she is free to leave whenever she wishes, though considering everything you lot have been keeping from her, she may not want to see any of you ever again."

"What did you tell her?" I growl, barely restrained anger making my voice shake. The driver glances at me from the rearview mirror before quickly returning his attention to the road and switching lanes to pass a transport truck.

Selene sighs as if I'm a child who stepped out of line, and it makes my jaw clench. "Relax, my love," she purrs. "She knows nothing, which I imagine is exactly why she's so upset with you and your boys."

"You don't know anything." I grip the edge of the seat until my knuckles are leached of color. My insides are on fire, and all I want to do is scream. Instead, I pull the phone away from my ear for a moment and suck in a slow, steadying breath. In a low voice, I say, "Tell me where you are, Selene."

"Hmm, now that is tempting."

I close my eyes against the tension building behind them and let out a sigh. She's taunting me, and I shouldn't have expected anything less. Even still, the way it still gets under my skin in seconds is infuriating. "What game are you playing?"

She laughs, and it's a soft, lyrical sound that I used to adore. Now it claws through me like nails on a chalkboard.

"Selene," I growl. I'm losing it; my heart rate has kicked up and my knee is bouncing quickly. The situation is slipping out of my control—that's if I had any to begin with, which when dealing with my sire is unlikely.

"It was lovely speaking with you, Gabriel. I can't tell you how much I've missed the sound of your voice, even when you're cross with me. I do hope to see you soon. We have so much to catch up on, you and I."

Before I can get another word in, the line disconnects.

The phone slips out of my fingers and bounces against the seat next to me. I snatch it up and shove it in my jacket pocket as the driver pulls through the gates leading to the airstrip.

After what felt like the longest flight of my existence, I'm back at home in Washington, sitting stiffly on the couch next to Kade. Lex and Atlas are in the chairs across from us.

"Now that we know who took Calla," Kade says, "we just need to find out where they are."

"Selene's got a witch blocking their location," I say, pinching the bridge of my nose as I lean against the back of the couch. "The only shot we have of tracking them is using the bond I have with her."

"You don't think she's blocking that as well?" Lex questions.

I shrug, flicking my eyes over to him. "Won't know until I try it." Tapping into that bond is the very last thing I want to do—I haven't done it in decades—but if it means getting Calla back, I'm going to shove aside all my shit and do it.

"You want us here, brother?" Kade asks, his eyes on me. There's tension in his forehead; he's worried about me, though he doesn't know the history I have with my sire, he— along with the others—can likely sense the unease coursing through me.

I exhale a heavy breath. "Yeah. I know I owe you all an explanation—"

"Stop," Atlas cuts in, shaking his head. "You owe us nothing. Understand?"

"We're here for you," Lex chimes in. "That doesn't come with strings. You tell us what you want and when you want. Your terms, Gabe."

Nodding, I swallow hard. "Let's get this over with," I finally say.

"Try to relax," Atlas tells me, giving me a knowing look. Because the thought of any of us relaxing right now is pretty fucking laughable. Not with Calla out there with a psychotic vampire who is as unpredictable as she is powerful. She and Atlas are fairly close in years, both having been born to vampire bloodlines three centuries ago. He understands the magnitude of being a vampire's sire—another thing they have in common, and something I've never experienced aside from *being* sired.

I close my eyes, taking several breaths to steady my heart rate and even out my breathing. I focus on each core group of muscles in my body, one by one, forcing them to unclench. It takes a good ten minutes before I'm able to connect with the level of calm I'm typically able to achieve in a minute or so.

The room is silent, save for the beating of our hearts and soft breathing. No one speaks, they don't try to interfere, they're just here for me.

I tip my head back against the cushion and exhale slowly, pushing my senses outward. My fangs extend to their full length, my gums throbbing almost painfully. I try to visualize the image of my sire—the memory of her long, ivory hair and brilliant silver eyes. Her alabaster skin and dark lips. Just as her form starts to materialize in my head, every muscle in my body locks, and I grunt at the wicked sensation of hitting a solid wall of nothingness and being blasted backward. My eyes fly open, and I bark out a curse, my nerve endings tingling with electricity.

Kade grabs my arm. "What happened?" His eyes are narrowed, but concern fills his face.

"I…" My voice fades as I turn my gaze to Atlas. "I don't know. I thought it was working. Then it was like I ran into a wall out of nowhere and something shoved me back." I shake my head, trying to clear the thick, heavy fog there. "Could she be blocking me herself?"

Atlas frowns. "I haven't heard of that. The sire bond is an open connection, from the moment it snaps into place until one vampire perishes."

I rub at my temples, willing the deep ache to subside.

"Then I have no idea what the hell just happened. I feel like she pushed me out." Shoving my hand through my hair, I get up, cursing again under my breath. Guilt weighs heavy on my chest, and the only way to make it fade is to get Calla back.

"We're going to figure this out," Kade says, looking up at me.

"How?" I practically growl. "You don't know her, Kade. She could be tormenting Calla every second that we don't find her. Messing with her head, *biting her*, telling her everything we've kept hidden to ensure her safety." I scoff, more to myself than at him. "And look where that got us," I grumble. "We have no idea what's happening to her, and this is my fault. Selene is trying to get to me by hurting Calla."

"Gabe, don't," Kade says in a firm voice, getting off the couch in a blur of movement and moving to stand in front of me.

"It's true," I snap. "I'm not strong enough to find out where she is."

Kade steps forward until we're nose-to-nose, and grabs my arms to keep me from moving away. "Yeah, and I was the one here when she left. How do you think I'm feeling about the situation?" His tone is sharp and there's a fire in his eyes that I know is reflected in mine.

I grip his arms, digging my fingers into his leather jacket. "She's in danger because of me," I say through my teeth, breathing hard. My heart is slamming against my ribcage with every painful beat.

Kade lets go of my arms and pulls free of my grip before cupping the side of my neck. "That's enough." His voice carries an authoritative tone I'm not used to hearing from him. He leans in, pressing his forehead to mine. It's cool against my fevered skin, and I shut my eyes, my pulse ticking unevenly.

"Kade—"

"Blaming yourself isn't going to bring her back, so quit it. We're going to find her." He tightens his grip on me, pulling me closer until our chests are pressed together. "Calla is going to come home, and we're going to kill the bitch that took her." He lowers his voice. "And who did this to you."

My chest tightens, and I pull away from him, walking around the couch. I head for the stairs leading to the second level. Lex calls my name, and I hear him move to follow me, but Atlas says, "Give him a minute."

I move with inhuman speed, not stopping until I'm in my bedroom, a closed door separating me from the rest of the world. I fall back against it, my hands clenched into fists at my sides and a muscle in my jaw ticking angrily.

I was our only chance, and I failed. If I'm to believe what Selene said on the phone, until Calla decides she wants to leave, we have no way of finding her.

❧ 6 ☙

## CALLA

My footprints have to be imprinted in the floor by this point. I've been pacing back and forth across the room for what feels like hours. I really shouldn't be using my energy where I don't need to, but I've never been this restless. My skin itches and my mind is spinning.

I take a hesitant sniff of my underarm and recoil at the less than pleasant smell. Frankly, I stink. The thought of showering is both enticing and exhausting, but when I try to run my fingers through my hair to pull it back and they get tangled immediately, my mind is made up. I'll shower and then come up with a way out of here.

Closing myself in the en suite bathroom, I flip the lock over, as if that will do anything, and push the thin black straps off my shoulders. I shimmy a little until the slip dress reaches my hips, then falls to the shiny white marble floor in a pile of silk, and I kick it away with a scowl. I pad across the smooth floor and open the massive glass shower door, then frown when I can't find the dial to turn the damn thing on.

"What the hell?" I step back, letting out an annoyed breath

when I find a touchscreen built into the wall. "You've got to be kidding me…" I cross my arms over my bare chest, staring at the screen for a few seconds as I pull my bottom lip between my teeth. I tap the screen a bunch of times until I finally figure out how to turn the hot water on. It cascades down from a wide-surfaced waterfall shower head, and I can't help but sigh when I step under the steaming spray.

I close my eyes and tip my head back, letting the hot water refresh me and ease the pounding in my head. I grab bottles and a loofah, scrubbing every inch of my skin until it tingles. The room smells of vanilla and roses, and the idea of staying in here forever is wildly enticing. Here, I can forget about everything. I can pretend for a short while that I wasn't kidnapped—*again*—and that I'm going to have to make Selene believe I've agreed to help her get Gabriel back if I want to make it out of this place.

My thoughts drift to the guys and what they're doing. In spite of being confused and angry as ever at the vault of secrets that seems to get more and more packed, there's a tugging in my chest. I don't want to, but I… I miss them. Lex's dry humor, Gabriel's softness, and Kade's flirting. Hell, I miss Atlas too, even with his constantly stoic and broody demeanor.

My fingers glide across my skin, brushing over the mounds of my breasts before heading lower. I keep my eyes shut, imagining I'm not in the shower alone. That instead, Atlas is here with me and it's *his* fingers teasing my skin as they get closer to the throbbing heat between my thighs. I pull in an uneven breath, leaning against the cool shower tile as I slide my hand down my stomach until my fingers reach my clit. I press my lips together at the bolt of electricity that shoots through me and trace the bundle of nerves at my center in slow, light circles, widening my stance slightly as water continues to shower down on me from above. Steam fills the room, making everything hazy and warm, and my breath becomes heavier. I dip a finger between my folds, sighing softly before quickly adding a second, imagining Atlas holding me back against the shower tile as he torments me with his fingers. I pick up the pace, circling my clit harder and faster with my thumb. Atlas wouldn't be gentle—he warned me as much—and that only spurs me on, my heart rate kicking up and pounding in my chest as pressure builds lower. I bite my lip to keep from moaning, thrusting my fingers harder, curling them at the deepest spot inside me until my knees start to shake. I lower myself onto the marble shower bench, spreading my legs as wide as they'll go, and resume thrusting. I climb higher and higher, all the while, picturing Atlas's dark gaze boring into mine as his fingers move inside me, hard and unforgiving, until an orgasm crashes into me, and I suck in a breath, pressing my free hand against my mouth to stifle the sound.

My cheeks and chest feel hot, almost feverish as I pull my fingers out, cleaning them before I turn off the water and stand on shaky legs to step out of the shower.

I wrap a towel around myself and walk over to the vanity, staring at my flushed appearance in the foggy mirror. *I can't believe I just did that.* But of all the crazy I've gone through in the last… however long I've been here, giving myself the release I desperately needed is probably the least crazy. I had a few minutes of peace and pleasure where I didn't have to think about the shitstorm I have an awful, gut-wrenching feeling I'm about to endure.

I dry my hair with another towel and walk back into the bedroom. In the closet next to the bathroom, I find a pair of black jogging pants and a heavy knit beige sweater—actively ignoring how creepy it is she has a closet stocked with clothing in my size—to tug on over my wet hair, which I manage to comb through after using about half the bottle of conditioner in the shower.

Taking a deep breath, I exhale slowly and open the bedroom door, stepping into the hallway. I peer around both ways, though the room I was in is pretty much at the end of the hall. I start walking the other way, the dark wood floor cold against my bare feet. The walls on either side of me are light gray and clear of any art, with ceilings that are high, lit with pot lights every couple of feet. There's a faint scent of bread in the air and the closer I get to the end of the hall, I start to hear soft music as well. I pause in the doorway, faintly recognizing the space from before Selene saved me from Dante... and then attacked me. My pulse jumps as my eyes flit to the spot on the floor Dante fell to in front of me, but there is no trace of what happened there.

"Oh, hello."

I jump at the timid female voice and whirl around to find an older woman with pale blue eyes staring at me.

*She's human.*

"I hope you haven't been waiting long," she says, glancing down to the black tray she's carrying. On top is a steaming dish of what looks to be some kind of stew along with a thick chunk of sourdough bread and a glass of water.

"I, uh... No." I shake my head for extra measure, wanting to reassure her that she's done nothing wrong. The thought of her being employed by Selene makes my skin crawl. She looks far too kind to be in this position, to be working for a vampire thirsty for power. Perhaps she doesn't know the truth about her employer. More likely, the poor human is glamoured.

The woman ushers me to the dining table and sets a spot for me, hurrying away before I have a second to thank her. It's not her fault I'm stuck here, so why shouldn't I be gracious toward someone showing me kindness? The way I see it, us humans have to stick together in this crazy super-natural world.

I take a seat and stare at the food for a few minutes. I'm aggressively *not* hungry, my stomach a swirling mess of nerves. But Selene was right about at least one thing—I need to eat something. I take a small sip of water before picking up the spoon and gingerly scooping some of the stew out of the dish. I lift it to my mouth and force myself to chew, swallowing slowly. I have no doubt whoever made it has cooking experience and uses only high-end ingredients—I wouldn't expect anything else from the vampire who lives here—but each bite I take tastes like dust and sits heavy in my stomach. It takes me a while, but I finish the entire dish, reminding myself with every swallow that I need to regain my strength.

I'm using the last bit of bread to soak up the remnants of the stew at the bottom of my dish when the soft *click, click, click* of heels echoes down the hallway. I glance up just in time to find Selene floating into the room, her fingers wrapped around a cup of tea. She walks over to the table and sits across from me, the subtle scent of peppermint wafting over from her steaming mug.

I finish off the bread, washing it down with the rest of my water, feeling more than a little awkward with Selene watching me silently.

Finally, she says, "I hope that was to your liking." Her tone is kind, almost as if we're friends. It's a laughable notion, one that also makes me drop my hands into my lap so she can't see me clench them into fists.

I offer a single nod in response, not bothering to look at her. Instead, I let my eyes wander across the intricate gold design of the table linen and listen to the soft jazz music still playing from behind a closed door nearby. In the kitchen, I'd guess, where the human Selene is most likely forcing to play housekeeper is probably doing dishes after serving my food.

Selene offers a small laugh. "Oh, come on, Calla. Your silence is absolutely deafening. Please say something. I suppose you might have more questions for me?" she offers. "Ask away. I'm an open book."

I lift my gaze to her face. "How much do you know about the deal my family made with Gabriel and the others?"

She purses her lips, regarding me with an amused look. "I'd venture a guess that I know far more than you do."

"Yeah, well, no one has really explained it to me in detail," I tell her. "Every time I ask, I get vague, non-answers."

She takes a sip of her tea, setting the mug down without making a sound against the table. "That must be incredibly frustrating."

I have the fleeting thought that I may not have the opportunity to ask anyone again, so I swallow past the sudden dryness in my throat and say, "Will you tell me what you know?"

She leans back a little, arching a brow at me. "Hmm. Will you agree to take the deal I put on the table earlier?"

My stomach drops. "I..." I look away, unable to hold her gaze as I force out the words. "I'm thinking about it."

There's a stretch of silence before she says, "Very well. I will share what I know of your bond with the vampires. Consider this your one free pass. I don't make a habit of giving without getting something in return."

I hold back an eye roll, knowing that will likely only result in her changing her mind about sharing information. Instead, I force out one low word. "Noted."

Selene presses her lips together as if she's making sure her lip color is still even. "How much do you know about the oath?"

I frown. "Stupidly little considering I'm the person it affects the most."

Her lips twitch. "Fair enough. Allow me to enlighten you."

She moves her hair over her shoulder, fixing her gaze on me. "Your ancestor, whoever it was—"

"My great-great-grandfather," I cut in.

She blinks at me, then continues as if I didn't speak. "He was trying to make a name for himself, to provide for his family. The man was convinced to make an investment in a company on Wall Street. Of course, he wasn't in a place financially to do this, but after being convinced it was so low risk and his return would essentially set his family up for life, he was prepared to use every dollar he had."

My heart is in my throat, and I haven't taken a proper breath since she started talking. Since I learned of the blood oath, I've been equal parts dreading and desperate to find out what really happened. Now it seems I'm about to, and I'm gripped with panic.

"What he didn't know was that the investment he was going to make would only benefit a few people—it was what's now known as a Ponzi scheme.

"Before the money went through, he was tipped off that it was a scam and the company he was investing in was tied to a lot of shady men."

"Dante?" I ask, chewing the inside of my cheek.

She shakes her head. "Dante worked for them. When your great-great-grandfather backed out of the deal, Dante was sent after him to shut him up permanently. They couldn't risk being exposed as a sham. The night Dante went after him, one of your guys—the tattooed one, I think—stumbled upon them. As far as I know, it was by accident. A complete coincidence."

"Wait. Lex is the one who saved him?"

She inclines her head slightly. "Dante has always been an arrogant prick. A popular opinion clearly, because Lex decided to interrupt and mess with him. Lucky for your ancestor, Lex wouldn't let Dante kill him."

"But why?"

She shrugs. "You'd have to ask him."

"Wh-what happened after that?"

"Dante took off, and the man thanked Lex profusely. When he offered Lex anything in return for saving his life—"

I suck in a sharp breath. "You have got to be kidding me."

"You know Lex better than I do," she offers with a light shrug. "He asked if the man had a daughter."

My jaw clenches, and I grab the glass in front of me, only to find it empty. I set it down a little too hard.

"He was confused and told Lex he had a son."

"Let me guess, then Lex said he wanted the firstborn daughter?"

"That part of the story you know."

My eyes burn, and I blink quickly to keep the tears at bay. I wasn't expecting to get so emotional hearing how everything went down. "So what? He just agreed to it?"

Selene purses her lips. "Not at first. He was confused and angry and utterly refused. Until Lex shared his little secret." She flashes her fangs. "When he told him the men he screwed over by going back on his investment were powerful and would continue sending people like Dante after him if he wasn't under the protection of people stronger than them, he didn't have much of a choice. Terrified for his family's safety, he reluctantly agreed and went with Lex to meet the others. And the rest is history."

I swallow hard, pushing my plate away. "Right." Shaking my head, I exhale a slow breath, trying to make my head stop spinning. "And what about Atlas's involvement with the Ellis family? Do you know about that?"

A small smile plays at her crimson lips. "What do *you* know?"

I narrow my eyes at her. "Literally nothing. That's why I'm asking."

"I'm not sure what Atlas is up to with them. Perhaps it's a matter of self-preservation."

My brows pinch together, and I can already sense the beginning of a headache forming in my temples. "I don't understand."

"Being a vampire and keeping the company of vampire hunters is generally not a smart idea, but I'm assuming there's more to it. Atlas isn't so arrogant he would risk his existence without good reason."

What. The. Fuck.

"Vampire hunters," I breathe, nausea coiling in my stomach. I grip the edge of the table, my knuckles turning white under the pressure.

"Ah. This is the first you're hearing of them," she guesses, and I don't bother responding. My reaction is obvious enough. "If I can offer you one bit of advice, Calla—assume everything you believe to be a myth is real. Because it most likely is."

I sit in silence, unable to form a coherent thought, much less an intelligent response.

"You could escape all of this," she says. "If you do as I ask, I can bring back your normal, vampire-free life. Consider what that would mean for you, Calla. You would never have to experience being taken advantage of by the supernatural again. Never glamoured or fed on by a vampire..." She sets her tea down and stands, walking around the table.

I track her movement, my pulse kicking up the closer she gets to me. Before I can attempt to move away, Selene shoots forward at a speed too quick to see and grabs a fistful of my hair in her grip. I cry out as white-hot pain sears across my scalp, and Selene yanks my head back, exposing my throat as she bares her fangs. I don't have a moment to yelp, to beg her not to bite me before she sinks her fangs into my throat.

A scream tears from my lips before she presses a finger

against them and the sound stops. My head spins in confusion and the rapid blood loss, and I faintly wonder if I'm being glamoured into silence.

Pain ripples through me like sandpaper in my veins, and I squeeze my eyes shut, screaming internally. I can't move, can't try to shove her back or pull away. Wetness tracks down my cheeks, and a whimper slips through my lips when her grip tightens for a moment before she pulls away from my neck.

When Selene steps back, licking my blood from her lips, I fall against the chair, my shoulders slumping with exhaustion. My eyelids flutter, fighting to stay open as darkness threatens to claim me. My vision ebbs in and out, and there's a dull ringing in my ears.

Selene speaks, but her voice sounds far away and muffled. "Hmm, perhaps now I understand why those boys keep you around." She flicks her tongue along her bottom lip, smirking at me. "You *are* delicious."

Nausea rolls through me as I grip the table in front of me until my knuckles turn white, pulling myself upright as best I can.

She says nothing more before turning and walking away.

I glare at her retreating form and grab the linen that came with my food, pressing it against the puncture marks Selene didn't bother to heal. It takes me at least three attempts to stand. My knees keep giving out, dropping me back into the chair. Tears burn my eyes, and I grit my teeth, hauling myself upright once more. This time, I'm able to stand. I use the table to walk, hesitating when I reach the end. There's still a good ten feet to the hallway without any support. I take a deep breath, putting one foot in front of the other until I make it there and fall against the wall. I manage to use it to make my way back to the room I woke in, closing the door behind me before shuffling to the bathroom where I collapse against the vanity. I stare angrily at the sickly pale reflection looking back at me. She is all too human. Weak.

I drop the bloodstained linen into the sink and back away from the vanity until I hit the closed bathroom door. My knees buckle, and I slide to the floor, pulling my legs to my chest. I bite my lip in an attempt to stop it from trembling, but my chin still quivers as my vision blurs with hot tears. I can't hold them back, not now that I'm alone. They fall down my cheeks, the lump in my throat quickly growing thicker, and the pit in my stomach heavier than ever.

For a moment, I miss how things were. Anything is better than this, including living in a mansion with four vampires who did anything and everything to keep me in the dark. Now, knowing… well, likely not everything, but a lot more than before, I have even more questions that are making my head spin. I shove a hand through my hair to push it away from my face and wince when my fingers brush the bite mark on the side of my neck. Having experienced both ways of being fed on—the pleasurable and the painful—I would take being bitten by one of the guys over another vampire any day.

I sigh and tip my head back against the door. My best friend's family are vampire hunters. Super inconvenient when I live in a house full of them.

As far as I know, Brighton has no idea what her family does. She doesn't know about vampires—Kade made sure of that when I told her about them. Either she honestly had no idea before I blabbed, or she was a damn good actor that day at the waterfront.

Chewing my bottom lip, I tear at the skin there, choosing to focus on the discomfort of that instead of the weight in my chest. I may have gotten answers to some of my questions, but those only prompted more questions. I still have no idea what the guys were planning before Dante swiped me off the street the other night, or how I would've been involved in it. I suppose that's a problem to address once I've made it out of the clutches of the psychotic vampire in the other room. But as it stands, I don't have a fucking chance against her.

## ❧ 7 ❧

## GABRIEL

When I was a new vampire, following my sire around like the lost puppy I was, we spent a short period of time in Washington, feeding our way through the city, from the seedy bars and nightclubs in the downtown core to a small bed and breakfast we spent one of our first nights together after I'd turned.

Of all the things I can remember from my time with Selene, I wish I could forget that night. We'd spent it drinking at a tiny, hole-in-the-wall pub not far from the B&B. It was long past midnight by the time we stumbled in for the night, of course waking every visitor in the place, as well as the owner. Instead of apologizing, which I immediately sought to do, Selene grabbed the guest closest to her and ripped into her throat.

The rest of that night is a blurry memory filled with terrified screams and blood. So much blood. I lost myself in it. The moment the crimson spilled onto the soft white carpet at my feet, my world narrowed on one thing—feeding.

Between the two of us, we tore through every human in the place. When we left the following morning, there were bodies littered all over the floor and staircase. Blood soaked into the carpet and hardwood, splatters going up the crinkled wallpaper in every room.

We had massacred two dozen humans for no other reason than entertainment.

My stomach roils at the memory; I've never told the guys the story of how I turned. They've gathered over our years together that it was less than voluntary, and they know who my sire is, but that's about it. I don't want them to know what I did or the monster I was. My reluctance to share has nothing to do with them—I trust them all with my life—and has everything to do with my own shame.

I give my head a firm shake to try and clear it. *I need to focus.*

Selene likely still has property in the vicinity, but even with my connections to the local government and law enforcement, I'm unable to track them down. By now, to protect herself from her growing list of enemies, any property she owns in the city is no doubt in someone else's name. I didn't consider myself one of her enemies—not until she came after Calla.

The four of us sit around the dining room table, drinking mugs of microwaved blood. It's taking the chill out of my bones, but that's about it. I still feel weaker than I ever have before. I scowl at the slight tremor in my wrist as I lower the mug to the table.

"We're going to find her," Lex says, and I flick a glance across the table at him. His usually bright white hair is faded and dull. It isn't styled—it's not even combed. It looks as if he got out of the shower, ran a towel over it, and called it good enough. He's wearing a wrinkled black hoodie, with darkness in his eyes that is mirrored on the others' faces as well. I'm sure my appearance is similarly dark and disheveled.

Atlas nods at Lex in agreement, wiping the blood from

his lip with the edge of his thumb. He turns his silver gaze to me. "And when we do, you don't need to worry. I will handle Selene."

The knots in my stomach give an uncomfortable, almost painful tug. As badly as I want to shred her porcelain skin to ribbons of flesh and muscle, sink my teeth into her throat and drain every last drop of blood from her body before ripping out her heart and burning it to ash, I *physically* can't. The born vampire that turns a human is protected against them should they ever turn on their sire. I can't bring harm to Selene. And while I can't be the one to bring an end to her miserable, murderous eternity, I will sure as hell be there to watch it come to fruition.

With her many years and powerful bloodline, Atlas is likely one of the only vampires we know that is strong enough to take her on, and he won't be doing it alone. Lex and Kade will back him up. Regardless of the fact he only turned Lex and not Kade or me, the four of us are bonded in a way unlike any blood oath or sire bond—by *choice*.

I nod, frowning at the pull of exhaustion in my muscles. I'm sure they're feeling it too. The blood we've consumed tonight wasn't fresh, and we're all suffering for it. "I don't want to make this about Selene. That's exactly what she wants. Let's just focus on finding our girl."

Atlas claps me on the shoulder from where he's sitting diagonally across from me at the head of the table. "We're going to get her back." His voice is deep and smooth, commanding. He says the words as if there's no other option, and something like hope flickers in my chest.

Kade props his chin on his hand, closing his eyes. "While we're all here, we should probably talk about our friends with the pointy murder devices."

I let out a heavy sigh. "Yeah, all right. When I talked to Marcel last, there hadn't been any new developments from his end to report. I'm assuming that is still the case, otherwise we would have heard from him."

"I spoke to my team in Vancouver about an hour ago. One of our guys intercepted some intel from Ellis Industries regarding a new site."

"Fuck," Lex grumbles, "they found more white ash?"

Atlas nods, his expression grim. "From what I can tell through company communications, they don't plan to start development until the summer."

"Let's burn it down before then," Kade suggests. "Problem solved."

"One of the lesser problems, unfortunately," Atlas says. "The number of hunters is steadily increasing across the map. Our only saving grace at this point is that they have to be more careful with how they're getting rid of vampires. In the age of social media, it's becoming rapidly more difficult to keep the existence of hunters—and vampires—secret from the general population. There's always someone around with a camera."

"Nothing stays secret forever," Lex says in a low voice, his eyes trained on where he's drumming his fingers against the top of the table.

I scratch the stubble at my chin; I still need to shave. "It's going to take a lot for Calla to forgive us... to trust us after keeping Brighton's family's involvement in our world from her." I'd never been particularly fond of keeping her in the dark, but it was necessary. We had no idea what she would do with the information—and she would've had no idea how dangerous that information was in the wrong hands.

I suppose it's too late now. She knows part of the truth at least. And whatever Selene tells her for her own personal gain. I force my jaw to unclench and glance around the table. "Perhaps it's time we show her a little trust?" I offer. "As much as we've asked of her anyway."

Kade tilts his head, looking at me with uncertainty in his tired gaze for a brief moment before nodding. "When we get her back, and we *will* get her back, I think it's time we tell her everything. No more secrets. She's a part of this now."

"She's a part of us," Lex adds.

Another look around the table, and it's clear we're all in agreement. Atlas's jaw is set tight and there's a familiar darkness in his eyes, but he nods, even if he isn't happy about it.

*No more secrets.*

❧ 8 ❧

# CALLA

The sound of tense conversation reaches me before I'm fully awake. Muffled, angry voices pull me out of bed, and I wince at the throbbing pain in my neck. I brush the sleep-tangled hair away and trace my fingers over the raised skin, biting my lip as I tiptoe toward the closed door. My movements are slow and hesitant as I wrap my fingers around the cool doorknob and turn it, tensing as I wait for the metal to creak and alert Selene to my presence. Letting out a breath when it doesn't make a sound, I open the door a crack and turn my head so my ear is positioned to hear what's being said from somewhere down the hall, likely the living room.

A gruff curse makes me jump, and my stomach clenches in the same moment my heart sinks as I recognize the male voice. It's Scott Ellis—Brighton's dad.

"You better watch yourself." Selene's voice slices through the silence, sharp and filled with venom. Hatred.

Scott offers a harsh laugh, as if he finds her threatening response to whatever he said to be pathetic. "We'll be in touch."

My brows knit in confusion, and a moment later, the front door slams shut, echoing through the place.

I close the door and lean against it, trying to come up with a reasonable explanation for Scott meeting with Selene. What would a vampire hunter be doing at the home of a born vampire *alone* and without trying to, you know, hunt them? It doesn't make sense.

With a sigh, I push away from the door and walk across the bedroom, slipping into the bathroom to freshen up before changing into a pair of black jeans and a maroon sweatshirt from the closet.

I comb my hair and finally leave the room, walking down the hallway with an uneven pulse and swirling nerves in my stomach.

Rounding the corner into the dining room and living room area, I find Selene lounging on the couch in front of a blazing fire, sipping what smells like coffee from a massive white mug. The half-full french press on the table in front of the couch beckons me closer, but the vampire guarding it keeps me back.

"Good morning," she says without giving any indication that she heard me approach. She keeps her back to me, cradling the mug in her hands, the matte red polish on her nails a sickening reminder of her brutal attack last night.

"Is it?" I blurt before I can stop myself and cringe, quickly recovering by adding, "I mean, that really depends on whether or not you're going to share that coffee."

She chuckles, finally turning her face to look at where I'm lingering near the hallway. "I suppose that's fair considering the drink I took from you last night."

My jaw clenches, and I bite my tongue to keep from saying something that will only get me in trouble. Instead, I force a smile and approach the seating area around the fireplace, picking the gray wingback chair, keeping as far away from Selene as I possibly can.

The moment my ass touches the chair, the human woman from yesterday hurries into the room with an empty mug, smiling warmly at me as she pours the coffee, setting the mug on the table in front of me.

"Breakfast will be ready shortly," she announces, turning her attention to Selene, and bows her head.

"Thank you," Selene says in a dismissive tone without looking at her housekeeper, and the woman retreats just as quickly as she came in.

I stare at the vampire over my steaming mug, my eyes narrowed as the warmth of the mug in my hand radiates through my fingers.

Selene scowls. "You can lose the judgy eyes, Calla. I compensate her very well for the work she does for me."

"Do you feed on her?" The words leave my mouth before I can stop them. My voice is barely above a whisper, but I have no doubt the vampire heard me.

"No." Her sharp silver eyes slam into me, and she drags her tongue over her dark red lips tauntingly. "I don't need to." Her words hold an unspoken threat that makes my chest tighten.

When she rises from the couch and walks to the dining room table, taking a seat at the head of it, I hesitate before following her. It doesn't take long for the human woman whose name I still don't know to bring out a steaming plate of seasoned potatoes with an omelet folded beside it and a colorful bowl of various berries. My stomach growls, but the savory smell has nausea rippling through me. I need to eat, to keep up what little strength I have, but the thought of picking up a fork and putting food in my mouth makes me want to bend over the side of my chair and vomit on the marble floor. I settle for pushing the food around my plate, forcing myself to swallow a berry every so often. It's not enough, but it's something. And considering my appetite is nowhere to be found since Selene tore into my throat yesterday, maybe I should give myself some credit.

Selene remains silent, sipping from a crystal glass of thick, dark red liquid.

Yeah, that sure as hell isn't helping my nausea.

"Have you given my offer any thought?"

Something in me cracks, and I drop the fork onto the plate in front of me, lifting my gaze to meet hers. "Do you know why they took me?" When she arches a brow at me, I shake my head. "Never mind, that was stupid to ask. Of course you do. That's why you thought getting me to turn on them would be easy, right?"

She purses her dark red lips. "Don't tell me you've made the mistake of caring for them?" Her tone is light, but there's a hint of slightly mocking disappointment there. Are we besties? Hell to the no. But that doesn't mean I want to see Gabriel stuck with Selene. I don't know the story of how he became a vampire aside from it being her who turned him, but if I had to bet—after my short time in Selene's company —the circumstances were less than ideal. As much as I want out of the arrangement that ties me to the guys *for as long as I shall live* or whatever, there has to be a better way. A way that doesn't damn Gabriel to an eternity with her.

"I didn't mean to," I admit, and I have no idea why.

She rolls her eyes. "You're overthinking this entire thing. Help me, and we can both get what we want. I know what you must think of me, but I do care about Gabriel. I turned him all those years ago to be with him forever. I never wanted to be separated from him... and those bastards—" She stops herself when the tone of her voice sharpens, then sighs softly. "They kept us apart for decades, and I want him back. I want my family back, Calla. Surely, you can understand that. Let's work together—this can be mutually beneficial. I want my old life back as much as you want yours."

I swallow the lump in my throat, my jaw clenched tight as I force back tears. Being offered something that would give me everything I want but that I can't accept hurts like nothing I've experienced before. I clear my throat, then say, "How could you break the blood oath anyway? I mean, theoretically?"

Amusement flickers in her gaze, giving me a brief moment to notice the shimmering dark blue shadow around her eyes, lined with a sharp cat-eye flick and long, dark lashes. "I've made many powerful friends over the centuries. Some of which have the power to sever the ties your blood has to the vampires who claim you."

I shake my head at her. "The power to sever a blood oath?" My stomach drops and unease prickles up my spine. "Like… magic?" The word is foreign on my tongue and sounds utterly ridiculous. So much so, I almost laugh.

Her lips twitch. "Don't look so surprised, Calla. Surely witches aren't too far of a stretch of the imagination once you've spent so much time with vampires."

I blink, trying—and failing—to wrap my head around her words. "I just… I hadn't considered that."

She offers a tight smile. "I can see that."

"Okay, so let's say I agree to your terms. You'll let me leave?"

Selene tilts her head to the side. "That's right."

"And you expect Gabriel to what? Just willingly leave his life behind and come join you?"

A chill races through me when the vampire smiles at me.

"He will," she says in a confident tone, "because if he doesn't, you'll be the one paying the price."

"You'll kill me," I say without missing a beat.

She purses her lips and runs her fingers through her hair idly. "Do you want to be a vampire, Calla?"

My brows knit in confusion, and I stare at her. "N-no." That avenue is not something I've ever let myself consider. My answer is more automatic than necessarily truthful, but I cling to it with everything I have, because the alternative… Becoming a vampire is just too damn terrifying to consider. Thinking about tomorrow is too overwhelming at this point. Toss eternity into the mix? No fucking way my mental state will survive that.

"Hmm." Her lips curl into a wicked smirk, as if my answer was exactly what she was expecting—and hoping for. "Then you will have Gabriel return to me. Otherwise, I'll turn you myself."

Panic clamps down on my chest, stealing my breath as my eyes widen. "You can't," I stammer. "I know how vampires are made, and I haven't—" My voice cuts off, and I clamp my mouth shut. She fed me her blood to heal Dante's bite marks and has been glamouring me all week. She could have easily forced me to drink it at any time, and I wouldn't remember. Bile rises in my throat, and I swallow hard. "Wh-what did you do?"

Selene rolls her eyes, managing to make even that look graceful. "No need for theatrics, Calla. Try to understand. I couldn't take any chances. I needed a contingency plan in the event you wouldn't take my deal." She shrugs, as if this whole thing isn't potentially life-changing for me. "So, you're going to go back to your little vampire hostel and tell Gabriel he needs to come back to me. So long as he does as he's told, you have nothing to worry about. My blood will work its way out of your system, same with the venom from my bite, and you'll be fine." Her voice lowers and hardens. "If he doesn't, there won't be a vampire on this earth who will be able to stop me from tracking you down and siring you to me. So really, it's either you or him." The corner of her mouth kicks up. "And no offense, but I'd much prefer him."

I press my lips together to keep them from trembling. "You are fucking insane," I seethe. "This is all some messed up game to you. This is my life. You're screwing with someone's life!"

"A game?" she breathes, a muscle feathering along her jaw as she traps my gaze with hers. Selene shakes her head. "I've told you why this needs to be done, and still…" Her fangs flash, extending to their full length, and I instinctively lean back from the table, my heart beating a little faster. In the time it takes me to blink, she moves, appearing beside my chair and hauling me up by the shoulder. The jerky, quick movement sends the chair to the floor, and I immediately fight to pull away from her. The moment she sinks her fangs into the delicate skin between my neck and shoulder, I scream. I can't help it. As much as I want to be strong and refuse to show weakness in her presence, the agony-filled sound rips through me before I can clamp my jaw shut. Ice fills my veins, but the spot Selene drinks from burns hotter than anything I've ever felt. I use every ounce of strength I have left and struggle against her, pulling hard, which only makes the feeding hurt far worse. Instead, I try pushing her away, but that gets me nowhere as dizziness crashes into me in waves, bringing with it a wicked nausea deep in my belly.

Selene growls at my struggle, shoving me back against the table. The blunt edge digs into my side, but I barely feel it. I put my arms back to catch myself, and my heart races when my fingers brush the knife next to my plate. I pick it up and swing blindly, praying it's enough to get her to stop drinking from me. If she takes much more, I'm going to collapse—and I might not get back up. I pull my hand back as she snarls viciously, then drops the blood-covered silver to the floor. The sound rings through my ears sharply, and I wince, the edges of my vision starting to blur and darken as I sway on my feet.

"You little bitch," she snaps, and her voice sounds as if we're underwater. Muffled and far away. As the wound quickly seals itself, she bares her fangs that are dripping with my blood; my attack did nothing but piss her off.

I open my mouth to say... what? I have no idea. But it doesn't matter. Before I can get a word in, Selene grabs me by the throat and slams my head into the table. Glass shatters and food goes flying. The room spins violently fast around me and every inch of my body hurts. Probably not as much as it should, which isn't a good thing. I'm starting to lose it, to go numb. I pull myself up, gripping the table to remain standing, and the second I catch my breath, Selene comes at me, backhanding me so hard across the face, my mouth fills with blood. I choke on it, spitting what I can onto the floor as I keel over, groaning. Sinking to the floor, my cheek presses against the cold marble. All I can smell is my own blood. The bitter, copper scent makes my stomach clench as my head pounds. Warmth trickles down the side of my face, and I don't have to reach up and touch it to know it's blood.

As my eyes start to close on their own, the pain ebbs away. The chill in my bones thaws, replaced by a soft, pleasant warmth.

I think this might be what dying feels like.

# 9

# GABRIEL

We all sense her at once.

Calla's presence returns just as quickly as it faded just over a week ago.

The four of us converge in the living room within seconds, but before we can get out the door, my phone chimes. With three sets of silver eyes on me, I pull it out and open the text.

"It's Selene," I say in a gravelly voice. "She says not to bother going after Calla. She's… she's heading to us anyway."

What the hell?

I shake my head, anger and confusion coursing through me at record-breaking speeds. A quick glance at the others tells me they're experiencing the same.

"She's just giving her back?" Kade says, crossing his thick arms over his chest. His eyes are narrowed and filled with doubt and suspicion. I don't blame him. He doesn't know Selene—none of them do. They don't know what she'll do to get what she wants—whatever the hell that is this time.

"That doesn't make any fucking sense," Lex adds, his

brows furrowed as he looks to me. "What game is she playing, Gabriel?"

I wish I had a better answer than the one I give. "Your guess is as good as mine. None of this makes sense."

Atlas remains silent, but the dark look on his face says it all. He's ready to go to war.

We take turns pacing the room while the others sit around, waiting. It's driving us all nuts, feeling her getting closer. The connection isn't as strong as it once was, which could be from her being away from us for so long. Magic is unpredictable that way.

Half an hour after the text from Selene, a town car with tinted windows pulls into the driveway. We're outside before the vehicle has a chance to shift into park, and Kade is a blur of movement, tearing down the stone steps and opening the back seat. The smell of her blood hits me, and every muscle in my body tenses. My gums throb as a growl rumbles in my chest before I move to stand beside Kade, sucking in a shallow breath at the sight of Calla, half-conscious and covered in her own blood in the back seat.

Lex curses in a sharp tone and moves toward the driver's door, but Atlas grabs his arm, pulling him back.

"He's human. Likely hired help." There's a warning in his voice. Translation: *don't kill the driver.*

Lex tears his arm away from his sire's grip and stomps off toward the house as Kade scoops Calla's limp, entirely too pale body into his arms and carries her inside. Atlas and I follow close behind. I steal a glance at him, wondering if he's struggling to not breathe in the scent of her blood as much as I am. The other two seem to be channeling it into rage. The thought of wanting to taste her blood again—right now of all moments—makes me sick to my core. I wholeheartedly despise the part of me I have to fight to keep control over. The part that wants to feed on the human Kade is laying on the couch with a gentleness I'm not sure I've ever seen from the vampire before.

She's barely alive.

My eyes scan the room, pausing on each of my brothers. There's a fire in Lex's eyes, but something else as well. He's scared—for Calla. Kade is sitting on the coffee table in front of the couch, stroking Calla's matted dark brown hair, brushing the messy waves away from her face. Under her eyes are dark, only made more prominent by her colorless complexion. Dried blood sticks to her chin, almost as if *she* was feeding, and my chest constricts at the thought. The front of her sweater is stained crimson, caused by blood running down her neck from the deep puncture marks there.

Atlas stands behind the couch, his arms gripping the back of it so tight his knuckles have gone white. His eyes are locked on her face, his jaw clenched tight.

"She's waking up," Kade says in a rough voice.

I move forward immediately, standing on one side of Kade, while Lex shifts to the other side.

Her eyelids flutter and her body tenses. When her brows pinch together and her chin starts trembling, I feel as if someone has stuck a hot poker through my chest.

She's in pain.

"Calla," Kade murmurs, cupping her cheek. His thumb brushes over her skin, as if he's trying to coax her awake. "Open your eyes for us. Please." That last word is a faint whisper, tinged with something awfully close to desperation.

I finally let out a breath when she opens her eyes. They're slits at first as she winces at the light above us. Lex quickly moves to shut it off. It's still daylight outside, which likely isn't helping.

"We should move her to the other room and draw the curtains. The sunlight—"

"I don't think we should move her," I cut in, unable to tear my eyes away from her frail body. "Not until she's healed."

Kade leans back slightly as Calla blinks her eyes open a bit more, then he bites into his wrist, moving to feed her—to heal her.

She stiffens, making a feeble attempt to move away from him before gasping for breath and collapsing against the cushions. "N-no," she stammers weakly, her voice raspy, *broken.*

The sound rips right through me, and guilt digs its claws deeper. This... Calla being in this pain is *my* fault. Selene intervening in her life, bringing this upon her... None of it would've happened if it weren't for me and my ties to the vampire who did this to her.

Kade's eyes narrow. "No? What do you mean, no?" He looks to me, then to Atlas, as if searching for direction. His expression softens as he looks back at her, and I know where this is heading. He's going to glamour her.

"Kade," she warns—not that it holds much strength. But he pauses, hanging onto her every word. "Please, no." She shakes her head, making it very clear she doesn't want his blood.

"Why not?" Lex asks, crouching in front of the couch to be closer to her. He slides his fingers through hers slowly, curling them around the back of her hand, his eyes searching her face.

Calla presses her lips together, flicking a glance toward where Atlas stands over her. Her brows pinch again and she lets out a shaky breath. "Selene bit me. More than once. Her venom is in my veins." She closes her eyes again, as if she can't bear to hold them open any longer. "And so is her blood."

"You drank her blood?" Atlas asks, speaking for the first time.

Her lips turn down. "No. I-I mean, yes." Tension fills her features, and she keeps her eyes shut. "I… I don't remember it. I didn't… even know it happened until Selene told me that she…" Her voice trails off and her eyes open, finding mine in an instant and knocking the air out of my chest.

I fight the urge to reach for her, to pull her against me and feel her heartbeat against my chest. To make sure she's really alive. "What did she tell you, angel?" I ask in a gentle tone.

She blinks quickly. "Gabriel, I…" She sniffles, struggling to hold my gaze. "I'm so sorry." Her chin quivers, but she continues, "If I die now, with her blood and venom in my system…"

Kade shakes his head. "Hey." He turns her face to meet his gaze. "That isn't going to happen. You're here, you're safe now."

"Safe." She chokes on the word.

"You need vampire blood to heal," Atlas says in a firm voice.

"What I *need* is for you to listen to me. For once." Her eyes flick between Kade's. "No more vampire blood. Just the thought of it makes me so nauseous my head won't stop spinning."

"Okay," Kade says.

I frown at the back of his head. That's it? We're just going to let her stay in this pain while her injuries heal at a human pace? My pulse kicks up, along with the throbbing in my gums as my fangs threaten to cut through. When a deep growl rattles through me, Atlas moves around the couch and grabs me by the arm, dragging me out of the room. He doesn't stop until we're in the formal sitting room, far enough away that Calla won't hear when I shove him away and snap, "What the hell was that?"

"You needed a minute," is all he says, standing between me and the hallway back to the other room.

"I need for her not to die," I correct him sharply.

He blinks at me. "She's not going to die, Gabriel. Take a breath and calm down. You getting worked up and pissed right the fuck off isn't going to help her. She will heal. Yes, far slower than if she drank our blood, but that's her choice. We're giving her that now, remember?" There's an edge to his voice that makes me think he's not finding it all that easy keeping it together right now either. He's certainly doing a better job at it than me.

"She'll suffer for what she did to Calla," I vow in a dark tone.

Atlas steps close again and claps me on the shoulder. "Yes," he agrees, "and it will be my pleasure to carry that out." He holds my gaze for a moment, then nods. "But for now, we need to take care of the human in the other room." He's right.

I inhale through my nose, pulling in a deep breath to try to center myself, then exhale slowly through my mouth. I nod at him before the two of us walk back to the other room to find Lex cleaning the blood off Calla's face and neck. Kade moved onto the couch in the few minutes we were gone and has Calla in his lap, her back against his chest and their legs stretched out in front of them while he strokes her hair.

Lex sets the bloodstained cloth down and helps her take a small drink of water before he moves out of the way, murmuring about making her something to eat as he heads into the kitchen across the room.

I approach at a calm pace, taking the spot Kade had been in on the coffee table before he moved to the couch with her. Calla's eyes follow me, and I lean forward, catching her chin gently, tilting her face up just enough that our gazes are level. "I need you to tell us what happened, angel."

She blinks at me, slowly registering my words. Her chin trembles as she opens her mouth to respond, then stops. Her jaw clenches against my fingers, and part of me fully expects her to yell, to scream at us for the secrets and lies.

Instead, she bursts into tears.

# 10

# CALLA

The tears come without warning. I've been trying so damn hard to keep them back, because I was terrified that once they started, I wouldn't be able to get them under control. And here we are. My shoulders shake with silent sobs, and I bury my face in Kade's chest, not wanting them to see me like this. The warmth of him, the steady beat of his heart against my cheek is grounding. And as much as I want to scream at them for everything they kept from me, the strength I'd need to do that isn't something I have right now. There's so much more I need to know—that *they* need to tell me, but for once, I'm glad they aren't just yet. I don't think I have it in me right now.

I use the back of my sweater sleeve to dry my cheeks. The tears slow, and I sniffle, staring out at the water in the pool as it glitters in the afternoon sunlight. I feel better, at least a little. The pressure in my chest from holding back the tears has eased, though it's been replaced by a pounding in my head—from the crying. I'm not sure where the tears came from, perhaps feeling relatively safe after not having a clue what was going on at Selene's triggered my body to release what I've been keeping locked up tight. Because, despite the lingering confusion and anger I hold with regards to the secret-keeping—especially about Brighton's family—I *do* feel safe here. With them. But it's moments like these, where that security makes me feel weak instead of strong, and I hate it.

Atlas disappears for a minute before returning, stopping in the kitchen and filling a glass of water before approaching the couch. He holds out the water glass in one hand and opens his other palm to reveal two white pills. "You should take these with food," he says pointedly but doesn't attempt to glamour me to eat something. Huh. Maybe I've finally made some progress then. Or he can tell by looking at me that the chances of vomit ending up all over the floor if he does force me to eat are too high to risk having to deal with.

I take the pills from his hand, then the glass. My hand shakes a little as I bring it to my lips and take a drink before tossing the pills back, followed by another mouthful of water to wash them down. I don't meet his gaze, nor do I thank him. Part of me wants to refuse the painkillers, but without them, the pounding in my temples is only going to get worse.

The five of us sit in silence for a while. I doze in and out of sleep, while Kade continues running his fingers over my hair. I'm clinging to the warmth of his chest against my back more than I care to admit—and I never will out loud.

When I open my eyes next, the sun is setting outside and Kade and I are alone. I rub my eyes and struggle to sit up, finally managing it with help.

"Easy, Calla," Kade murmurs.

"Wh-where is everyone?" I turn to look at him, my eyes tracing the hard lines of his face as I itch to reach forward and run my fingers along his jaw. Softness fills his silver gaze, along with a flicker of concern as he watches me, his dark hair falling across his forehead.

"Atlas is in his office and the others went out to pick up

food for dinner and a first aid kit." His fingers brush along my neck, making me shiver as he reaches the marks Selene left on me.

"Not used to needing that, I suppose," I say, lowering my gaze, wanting to close my eyes against his gentle touch.

He laughs softly. "Yeah, not so much." He cups my cheek, tilting my face back up. "How are you feeling? No bullshit."

I blink my eyes open. "Better, I think." The splitting headache is gone, and I don't feel as if my chest is going to explode from the pressure building inside me. My muscles still ache, but I imagine that will last for some time, same with the cuts and bruises I sustained at Selene's hand. But I'd much rather deal with that than risk drinking vampire blood right now.

Kade nods. "Good. Are you hungry?"

I press my lips together. The thought of food doesn't immediately make me nauseous, so that's a step in the right direction. "I can try to eat something."

"Glad to hear it." His fingers slip away from my cheek, and he taps the tip of my nose. "Gabriel mentioned making risotto. Think you'd be up for that?"

I nod, then shift away so I'm not pressed right against him. Sitting up, I slowly drop my legs over the edge of the couch, planting my stocking feet on the floor. I brace my hands on either side of myself and take a deep breath.

"Where do you think you're going?" Kade asks in a gentle tone before I can attempt to stand.

I sigh. "I need to get out of these clothes. Should probably shower too." I feel gross, and there's definitely blood dried into my hair.

In a blur of movement, Kade is in front of me, leaning down and sliding his arm around my waist, guiding me up until I'm standing. My balance is slightly off, so I'm glad he's there to lean against, but I feel ridiculous needing his help just to get off the couch.

"There you go," he says softly in my ear.

"You going to help me in the shower too?" I try to joke. "Wash my hair and everything?"

He doesn't miss a beat. "You say that like I won't." Kade lowers his face, pressing his lips against my hair. "Or are you thinking about the last time I took you in the shower?"

My face flushes, and I close my eyes. "Evidently, *you* are."

He chuckles, then kisses my cheek. "Always. I'm never not thinking about the next time I'll get to have you." His grip on my waist tightens. "But I don't think you're ready for that yet."

No. I suppose I'm not.

Kade helps me to my room and into the bathroom, where he pulls my pants down until I can step out of them as I hold onto his shoulders. I lift my arms over my head, wincing at the ache in them, and he quickly pulls my sweater off, dropping it on the floor. He lifts me onto the vanity without any effort, leaving me sitting there for a few seconds while he turns on the shower and pulls out fresh towels, setting them next to me. His hands find my thighs, warming my bare skin while steam fills the room around us, but his eyes don't wander. He holds my gaze, those bright silver eyes flicking between mine.

"What?" I ask in a low voice, my cheeks filling with heat.

The corners of his mouth curve up. "I'm glad you're back."

I blink in surprise. I'm not sure what I was expecting him to say, but apparently not that. "I..." I can't say it back. Because as much as I'm glad not to be locked up with Selene, I still have a lot to work through with the guys before I get to a place where I'm glad to be here.

"It's okay." He reaches up and tucks my hair behind my ear. "We have a lot to discuss—when you're ready."

My brows pinch closer. "We do?" I ask, hoping he'll offer more than that.

Kade nods, then lifts me off the counter, keeping his hands on my waist even after my feet are planted on the floor. "When you were gone, the four of us agreed it's time. No more secrets."

I drop my gaze so he doesn't see my eyes widen. "Oh." I'm finally going to get some answers, to understand what's truly going on here. It's what I want, and yet, there's a newly forming pit in my stomach telling me that I might not be ready for it.

"Do you want me to help you into the shower?" he asks.

I meet his gaze again. "You're asking this time?"

He smirks. "Yeah. Don't get used to it. I'm being nice because you're all sad and hurt."

I laugh—actually laugh. It's the first time in… I can't even remember how many days. The sound of my own laugh is foreign to my ears. "You're such a gentleman," I remark dryly.

He tweaks my chin. "We both know that's not true." He glances toward the shower before looking back at me. "You're good then?"

"You'll hear if I fall on my ass."

Kade leans in and presses his lips against my cheek. "Take your time and holler if you need me."

I nod silently and watch him leave the room, pulling the sliding door shut. With a deep breath, I step away from the support of the vanity and slowly make my way into the shower, where I proceed to spend the next hour washing every bit of me until I finally feel as if I might have cleaned the time I spent with Gabriel's sire off my skin.

Showered and dressed in my own clothing, I feel significantly better. The hot water eased the aches and pains in my muscles, and the fog in my head seems to have mostly cleared. I think I'm even a little hungry.

I walk out of the closet and freeze when I step into the bedroom and find Atlas standing in the corner, looking out the window with his back to me. My eyes immediately go to the door to the hallway, finding it shut. "What are you doing?" I finally ask.

Atlas turns to face me, and even from across the room, his dark silver gaze does things to me I don't want to think about. Because I am still very much pissed at him, and despite thinking of him while I was trapped at Selene's, I find myself fighting the urge to scream at him.

"Waiting for you," he says in a tone that suggests his answer is quite obvious.

My eyes narrow. "And you felt the need to do that in here?"

He crosses the room at an unhurried pace, closing the distance between us as he says, "Considering I own this house, I can do whatever I like, *wherever* I like."

I fold my arms over my chest, refusing to back away even when he stops so close I can feel his breath against my forehead. I stare at his chest, the sharp, black V-neck shirt he's wearing. "What do you want, Atlas?"

"Right at this very moment?" He snags my chin before I can turn away and forces my gaze up to his. "I'd like to wring your neck for taking off, for running away instead of facing what you found."

My brows shoot up as anger flares to life in my chest. I smack his hand away and step back, glowering at him. "Excuse me?"

A muscle ticks in his jaw, sharp and shadowed with stubble. "What you did was idiotic and immature and very well could have gotten you killed."

My voice trembles as I snap, "Fuck you." If this asshole thinks I'm going to stand here and let him blame *me* for the shit that's gone down, there's no way in hell that's happening.

His lips curl into a scowl. "Glad to see you haven't lost your fire."

"Get out."

"No, I don't think I will," he says in an annoyingly calm voice.

I let my hands fall to my side. "Fine. Stay as long as you'd like, *I'll* go." I move to shove past him, but he catches my wrist and pulls me toward him. When I stumble, falling forward into his chest, he takes that opportunity to back me up against the wall. He drops my wrist, caging me in between his arms and pressing his hands flat against the wall on either side of me. His expression is dark, vicious. I'm prepared for him to rip me apart, quite honestly, and my heart is hammering against my ribcage waiting for the storm to come.

"You," he starts in a low, deep voice, leaning down so his lips are at my ear, "have no idea what I would have done if something had happened to you."

The air is stolen from my lungs in a swift *whoosh*, and I suck in a breath, my heart in my throat. "Atlas," I say in warning, sinking my teeth into my bottom lip. The emotional rollercoaster that is this exchange isn't one I'd like to continue riding.

"I want to lock you up and never let you leave this house." He leans back to look into my eyes. "And I could."

I shake my head. "If this is your way of apologizing for keeping me in the dark, which pretty much led to me being kidnapped and used as a human juice box by not one but two psychotic vampires, you're doing a shit job."

"I'm not apologizing," he says flatly.

My jaw clenches at his tone. "Then what *are* you doing?"

Atlas cocks his head to the side, watching me. "Whatever I want."

I slam my palms against his chest, trying to push him

away, but he doesn't budge. Not a fucking inch. "Get away from me."

"Want to try that again with a more convincing tone?" he taunts.

Instead of fighting him, I lean back against the wall, exhaling harshly. "Not really. Want to stop being an asshole?"

He leans in for a moment. "Not really."

I roll my eyes, wishing I could make him feel as out of control as I do. "I thought of you," I blurt, "while I was there. About how angry I was for everything you kept from me, but… also how much I wanted you there."

His eyes dance across my face. "Oh?"

I swallow hard, forcing myself to look at him head-on as I say, "When I was in the shower, fucking myself to feel something, *anything* that could help me escape my reality, I closed my eyes…" My voice trails off as I close my eyes now, then continue, "and when I pushed my fingers inside, I pictured it was you there, thrusting into me while you held me against the wall."

Atlas growls deep in his throat. "What are you doing?"

My eyes fly open, and I arch a brow at him. "Whatever I want," I say, adopting his words.

"Hmm." He drops one hand off the wall, wrapping it around my hip. "And what is it you want, Calla?"

Leaning into his touch instead of trying to push him away, I lick my lips. "What I want?" I echo. "How about the truth? Kade said—"

"I don't care what he said," he cuts me off.

I scowl. "Of course not, because you—"

Atlas seals his lips over mine before I can finish my sentence. For a second, I'm lost in the taste of his lips, the way they move against mine, firm yet unhurried.

I shove him back, and my palm cracks against his cheek.

He blinks at me, surprise filling his eyes as he lifts his

fingers to his cheek, which is tinged pink where I slapped him.

My heart is pounding in my chest as we stare at each other in silence. And then I'm reaching for him, grabbing the front of his shirt in my fist and tugging him back to me. I lean up on my tiptoes and smash my lips against his, putting everything into the kiss. Every bit of anger and hurt at him for all of the secrets and lies, the fear I felt when Dante ambushed me on the street outside Brighton's apartment and being kept by Selene, and lastly, the bitter relief I feel being back here.

He grips my hips, hauling me flush against him and pressing me back into the wall at the same time. When he nips my bottom lip, I gasp into his mouth, and he growls in response.

I lean back, resting my head against the wall as I catch my breath. "I hate you," I say, my voice trembling.

Atlas smiles slowly, and my breath catches. It's the first time I've seen him smile. He has a small dimple in his left cheek when he does. He lowers his mouth, brushing his lips on mine. He doesn't kiss me, though. Instead, he whispers, "By all means, hate me for as long as you can, Calla. I'm still going to make you come."

I want to refuse him, to deny that I want what he's offering—*threatening*. But I can't. Even if I say the words, he'll see right through me. Atlas has intimidated and intrigued me from the moment we met, and as much as I wish I could say I don't want him, that I'm not drawn to the out of control way he makes me feel, I'd be lying to both of us if I did.

"Go ahead," he adds, lowering his voice, "tell me you don't want it."

My eyes narrow. "You're an asshole." It's a weak retort, but it's all I can come up with.

He chuckles, turning his head slightly toward the door.

"Yes, well, as much as you'd like this asshole to have his way with you, it sounds like Gabriel and Lex are back, so we'll have to pause our little tiff for now." Without so much as a glance at me, he turns and walks out of the room, leaving the door open so I can watch him retreat down the hall.

I fall back against the wall with a heavy sigh, pressing my hand against the pounding heartbeat in my chest.

*What the hell just happened?*

Lex and I are putting the last of the groceries away when Atlas comes into the kitchen looking rather... bothered. When I arch a brow at him, he simply shakes his head, shoving his hand through his hair, flexing the muscles in his forearm before dropping onto the couch in the living room. A minute later, the TV clicks on and the soft sound of the local news station fills the silence.

Calla walks in a minute later, her cheeks tinged slightly pink and her jaw set tight.

I want to ask what happened while we were gone, but whatever it was is between her and Atlas.

Her eyes move from me to where Atlas is focused on the screen in the other room. She lets out a little huff before turning her attention back to me. "I, um, need to talk to you."

The sound of her pulse increases, and I nod, shutting the fridge door. "Of course, angel," I say in a soft tone. "Maybe after some food? Are you feeling well enough to eat?"

She presses her lips together."I'm okay. I... I don't think this should wait any longer."

Lex is across the kitchen, pouring the contents of a

blood bag into a glass. "This sounds like something we should discuss together," he chimes in, tossing the empty blood bag in the trash under the sink and coming to stand next to me.

"Probably," she says, stealing another glance toward Atlas. "Where's Kade?"

The moment his name leaves her lips, he appears behind her, close enough she must feel his body there.

"Wherever you want me," he says in her ear.

She yelps, whirling around to face him, and drives her fist into his stomach. "Damn you." Her voice is a little breathless as she scolds him.

Kade grins at her. "Aww, come on. You know you missed me sneaking up on you." He dives down and plants a kiss against her cheek before she can shove him away, but a smile tugs at my lips watching her try.

Atlas takes that opportunity to get off the couch, shut off the TV, and join the rest of us in the kitchen. Lex immediately offers him the glass of blood in his hand, to which Atlas just shakes his head. Lex shrugs and takes a long drink. My gums throb watching the dark crimson liquid slosh around the glass.

I swallow past the fire in my throat and turn my attention back to Calla, who has moved away from Kade and is leaning against one of the islands.

She pulls her bottom lip between her teeth, hesitating.

My chest tightens, wanting to go to her, to wrap my arms around her waist and hold her close. The desire to reassure her that everything is okay is strong. It's a pull I'm struggling to ignore, because I get the feeling based on her response to Kade, that she needs some space. So, as badly as I want to crush her against my chest and make her feel secure, I keep my distance. Because there's also a part of me that longs for her blood, to feel her writhing against me, if the throbbing in my gums and the hardness between my legs are any indications.

Calla opens her mouth to speak, her eyes wider than normal as they bounce between all of us. When nothing comes out, she snaps her lips together, then clears her throat, trying again. "I have a lot to tell you. I know you're going to be pissed, but please let me finish before you say anything or have some supernatural meltdown."

Lex downs the rest of his blood in a matter of a couple gulps, setting the stained glass on the counter behind us. "What does that mean?"

She looks at him and sighs. "Just… I need you to listen, okay?"

I manage to catch her gaze and offer a reassuring nod. "Of course. We're listening."

She inhales deeply, then starts talking quickly. "The night I left here after finding those pages in Atlas's office, I went to Brighton's. Before I made it inside, Dante grabbed me off the sidewalk and knocked me out. I woke up in some fancy penthouse—I'm still not sure where it was—and he was there. I thought he took me as revenge against you guys for the Wall Street deal, but I quickly found out he wasn't the one behind it. Not really. He, uh…" Her voice breaks off, and she blinks a few times, trying to fight back tears. Swallowing hard, she continues, "He bit me. It was the worst pain I've ever felt. I mean, up to that point."

"He's a dead man," Lex growls, his fangs on full display.

Calla laughs, but the sound is void of any humor. "He *is* dead. So you can put your fangs away, Lex."

"Dante is dead?" Kade asks, crossing his arms over his chest.

She nods. "I thought he was going to kill me. And then, he just stopped." Her jaw clenches. "He dropped dead, after she, um—after Selene ripped out his heart." She shakes her head.

"I thought she was saving me from him," she says quietly, and her low voice makes me think she's beating herself up more than we know.

"What happened after that?" I ask, my stomach already churning at the mention of my sire.

Calla's brows pinch together as if she's struggling to remember. Her gaze drops to the floor, and she says, "I don't really know. She came at me, then everything went dark. When I woke up next, it was a week later, though I guess I'd been awake before then and don't remember it. She fed on me twice between the time I woke up and when she put me in a car to come back here." A shudder ripples through her as she seems to relive the memory of Selene biting her, and my hands curl into fists at my sides.

Kade growls low in his throat, and Atlas shoots him a warning glare that says, *keep it together*.

"I don't know what the hell is going on with Brighton's family," she says in a more level voice, lifting her gaze to look at Atlas, "but Scott was there. He met with Selene one morning. I don't know what they were talking about, but he left abruptly and it didn't seem good."

Atlas's eyes narrow. "You didn't hear *anything* they said?"

"Not really. I caught the end of their conversation. She sounded pissed, and he told her they'd be in touch."

"Well, fuck," Lex mutters. "Add that to our list of problems."

Calla frowns at him. "I wish that was it." Her eyes flick to me for a split second before they move away, her pulse jumping.

"What else is there?" I ask, that wretched pit in my stomach growing bigger by the second.

"As you could probably guess, she didn't send me back to you out of the goodness of her heart."

*Because she doesn't have one.*

"She wants something in return," Kade guesses.

Calla nods, her heart hammering in her chest as sweat dots her brow. "She…" Her eyes land on me again, glassy with unshed tears. "She wants you, Gabriel."

My stomach sinks. I'm not surprised—Selene has never been subtle or coy about what she wants—but the thought of returning to her, to even seeing her face, makes me sick. I can count on one hand the number of times in the last century I've vomited, but the bile rising in my throat threatens to increase that tally.

"At first, she wanted me to choose to convince you, but I refused her. As angry and confused as I was—as I *am*—I could never do that to you." She sucks in a breath. "She took matters into her own hands and decided to make you choose —you or me."

"What the fuck does that mean?" Kade demands.

She doesn't take her eyes off me as she says, "If Gabriel doesn't go back to her… she… she's going to turn me into a vampire."

"No fucking way," Lex snarls, his eyes dark. "She's not getting anywhere near you ever again. We're going to rip her limb from limb and set them on fire until she is nothing but ash."

Memories of my life before I met the guys flash before my eyes. The dark period I spent with Selene, the hunger and the bloodshed that followed everywhere we went. The thought of returning to that life grips me with a fear so strong my lungs constrict, making it hard to breathe. But if this is what it takes to keep Calla safe—

"I'll go." The words leave my lips before I realize I've spoken. The pit in my stomach seems to grow blades, slicing through my abdomen and filling my veins with poison that makes me bite back a string of expletives. I know this isn't ideal—for anyone—but I also know what Selene is capable of. I've seen it firsthand, and this is the least of it. So there isn't a choice here, not really. I have to do what she wants.

Kade moves forward, stepping in between me and Calla. "Absolutely fucking not. There is no way in hell we're letting you go back to that psychotic bitch."

Atlas steps up, standing next to Kade. "He's right. We will deal with Selene and we are more than capable of protecting Calla."

Calla scowls from behind Kade. "I want to be able to protect myself, thank you very much."

Atlas glances over his shoulder at her. "Fine. Once you're fully healed and have your strength back, we'll start training again. But don't think I'll go easy on you."

"When have you ever?" she shoots back, and there's a fire in her eyes that despite the fire blazing through me makes my chest fill with pride. Our girl is strong—oftentimes stronger than I think we give her credit for. It's one of many things I admire about her… and the thought of walking away from that and into the arms of the monster who created me has my thoughts moving toward a white ash stake to the heart.

Before I can speak, Calla says, "I'll agree to waiting to train on one condition."

Atlas offers a dry laugh. "There you go again thinking you have any choice in the matter."

Her usually soft, warm brown eyes darken as they narrow on him. "You're not the only person who could train me." Her gaze moves to Kade—specifically the bulging muscles in his arms.

Kade smirks when he realizes she's looking at him. "Oh no. Don't drag me into this."

She rolls her eyes, huffing out a frustrated breath. "I'm not asking for much here, guys."

"What *are* you asking for?" Lex asks.

"Answers. Honesty. *Transparency.*"

I glance between the guys, shrugging. We'd been planning to bring her into the fold anyway. This doesn't seem like a stretch. She deserves to know about the world she's living in.

"I want to know everything," she adds in a firm voice, looking at each of us.

Kade tuts his tongue. "Always so stubborn."

She shoots him an annoyed look, which does nothing to diminish the smirk on his lips as he watches her.

Kade glances in Atlas's direction, waiting until he nods to start talking. "Your BFF Brighton's family are vampire hunters."

Calla frowns. "I know that part."

"You also know that before we came for you, we spent some time—"

"Stalking me," she cuts in. "I do recall that part being mentioned, yes."

I frown at the bitterness in her tone and the tension in her body. Seeing her upset doesn't sit well with me. But we all agreed she deserves to know everything, and she's asked for transparency. She's entitled to any response she feels like.

"We gathered information on the people you spent time with," Kade continues. "Brighton included. We knew her relation to the hunters and very quickly deduced that she was not involved with the organization. From what Atlas could gather, Brighton's mother refused to allow her daughter to be a part of it. She didn't want that life for her."

"I met with Brighton a month before we came to your apartment," Atlas says. "I confirmed she had no prior knowledge of hunters or vampires or anything supernatural."

"So her reaction that day when I told her about you guys was genuine," Calla muses, her brows pinched together.

Kade goes on to reiterate the information we've already discussed about the hunters. That they're growing in numbers and that white ash may not be as rare as it used to be.

"What are we going to do about that?" she asks.

Lex chuckles. "You're going to focus on building your strength during training with Atlas and finishing the semester. You've always been adamant about school. Let us worry about this and you worry about that, okay?"

She blinks at him, and for a moment, I'm not sure if she's surprised by his suggestion or pissed that we're attempting to sideline her from the hunter action. Either would make sense at this point.

"Fine," she finally says, "but once school is done for the term—"

"We'll revisit this conversation," Kade says, adopting Atlas's firm tone.

Her eyes narrow on him and a muscle ticks along her jaw. She opens her mouth as if she's about to start arguing again.

"Okay," I say before the two of them can get into it in the middle of the kitchen. "I need to speak with Marcel—update him on the situation. Lex, can you start dinner? I shouldn't be long."

He nods, grabbing his empty glass off the counter and sticking it in the dishwasher before walking to the fridge.

I take that opportunity to slip out of the room, walking into the formal living room at the side of the house and perching on the stiff armrest of the couch. It's no wonder we never use this space—the furniture is most definitely for show and not comfort.

Marcel answers my call on the first ring.

"What's up, Gabe?"

"We've got her back," I tell him. "She was pretty banged up, but she's going to be okay. She already wants to start training with Atlas. We'll keep her safe, but she doesn't like feeling vulnerable, like she can't protect herself."

"Makes sense," he says.

"Yeah." I understand where she's coming from. I'd feel the same if I was in her position, I'm sure of it. "It was Dante that took her, but Selene was behind it."

"Son of a bitch," he says, sighing. "How'd you find her?"

"We didn't," I say reluctantly. "Selene sent her back to us." I fill him in on everything Calla told us, from Dante being dead to Brighton's dad meeting with Selene. "Things could get very messy. I want advanced security measures put in place around here."

"Of course. I'll arrange it immediately." The sound of laptop keys clicking fills the line for a few seconds. "Everything will be set up within twenty-four hours."

"Thank you, Marcel."

"Anytime, my friend. I'm glad your girl is safe."

Something in my chest tightens, and I press my lips together for a moment. "Me too."

"I've got a few calls to make, but I'll send you a confirmation email later once the security is set up. Let's plan to catch up in a few days, but if you need anything prior to then, you know where to find me."

After hanging up with Marcel, I rejoin the others. Lex is reading the instructions for mushroom risotto on his phone, while Atlas, Kade, and Calla are sitting in the living room.

The grim expression on Calla's face is quickly explained when I hear Atlas explaining his involvement in Ellis Industries.

"You're a shareholder in a company whose mission statement might as well be *kill all the vampires?*" She shakes her head. "What the hell?"

"It's important to keep our eyes on all of the moving parts when it comes to the hunters," Kade tells her. "Atlas being inside the company is the best way to do that."

"So long as you don't get caught," she says, directing it

toward Atlas. There's worry in her gaze that he seemingly ignores, though I know he sees it as clearly as I do. She shakes her head. "I thought it was an environmental company."

"It is," Kade says, "sort of. They are deeply involved with the protection of certain lands."

"Land where white ash trees are plentiful," I say, walking into the living room and sitting next to Calla on the couch.

She frowns, her eyes flitting between us as she puts it together. "They protect the land where white ash trees grow so they can use them against vampires."

"That's right," Kade says.

Calla runs a hand over her face, and I quickly notice the way her fingers are shaking. "This..." Her voice trails off. "This is insane." Her gaze focuses on Atlas. "You can't—What if they find out who they're in business with?"

He shrugs. "Keeps things interesting."

The muscles in her jaw tense. "I'm serious," she snaps at him.

Atlas sighs as if this whole conversation is an inconvenience to him, and I shoot him a look. "Nothing is going to happen, Calla. They aren't going to find out."

She crosses her arms over her chest. "Really? Because Selene knows about you *and* she knows Brighton's dad. There is absolutely no way that's a coincidence."

"Selene is also a vampire," he counters. "She wants to throw us under the bus, she's getting run over as well."

"That's what you're counting on?"

There's a slightly, barely noticeable shift in Atlas's posture. His patience is wearing thin. I understand Calla's concern—it's nothing I haven't been worried about before, but it's really not the most present issue.

I reach over and wrap my hand around her knee, giving it

a reassuring and gentle squeeze. "Everything is going to be all right, angel."

She glances down to where I'm holding onto her and purses her lips before meeting my gaze. "That's not... I just—"

"Trust us." I lower my voice. "Please?"

Calla catches her bottom lip between her teeth, and the urge to lean in and tug it free so I can seal my mouth over hers pulls at me, but I shove it down—for now.

Closing her eyes, she whispers, "I'm trying."

I glance over at Atlas and Kade, who both nod at me.

She's trying. That's really all we can ask for at this point.

## CALLA

My best friend's family is full of vampire hunters.

I lean forward, my elbows digging into my knees, and rake my fingers through my hair. My throat is thick with tears—again—and my head is so light, I'm glad I'm sitting down, otherwise there's a good chance I'd fall on my ass.

I've finally gotten the answers I've been asking for since day one, but I'm finding it all harder to swallow than I was expecting. At least they're being truthful and letting me in on what's going on. Honesty is what I need to help build my trust with the guys, and they are making a significant effort to give me that. It's not lost on me.

"What happens now?" I ask, sitting upright. "I've missed school—people, including Brighton, are going to wonder where I am."

"I dealt with Brighton," Kade says.

Cringing outwardly, I hesitate before asking, "What does that mean exactly? What did you do?"

He rolls his eyes. "Relax. After you seemingly went AWOL, she freaked out and called us. When Gabriel and I went over there to talk to her, I glamoured her to delete and forget about your texts. I also told her you were sick and would be out of commission for a while."

I let out a breath. I guess it could be worse. Except… "How am I supposed to act around her now?"

"Normal?" Lex offers from the kitchen. He's stirring something in a pot on the stove but shoots me a wink over his shoulder.

I stare at him. "That's helpful. Thank you." A pit grows in my stomach. "I know what you said about her mom not wanting this life for Brighton, but do you think they could be planning to use her in the future?"

"It's a possibility, of course, but they tend to start hunters much younger than she is so they can train for years before being used in the field."

I shake my head, still struggling to grasp this revelation. "Vampire hunters," I say in a low voice. "Don't you think their existence is something you should have told me about, I don't know, when I moved in?"

"We're telling you now," Kade chimes in, glancing at something on the phone in his hand.

I huff out a sigh. Maybe I should be more accepting of their newfound willingness to share things with me instead of dwelling on all of the time they kept me in the dark. "Okay," I say, leaning against the back of the couch and crossing one leg over the other. "What's the plan?" I need more to go on; it seems with every answer I'm given, it sparks a dozen more questions.

"We're still gathering information," Atlas says. "It's important not to move too quickly in order to stay undetected within the ranks of the organization."

"Right," I say, dragging the word out, clearly not sure what the hell he means.

"Atlas has a responsibility to help ensure the protection of our kind. The York family is very important in the vampire world. They go back centuries and are one of the most powerful and respected clans to exist."

"That explains a lot," I mutter under my breath.

"Watch it," Atlas says sternly.

"As you can see," Kade says, "our boy here doesn't love the attention being on him."

My lips twitch. I can't help it. I understand the situation is serious, but the small break in tension is appreciated. Despite that, my head still feels as if it's going to explode from all of this new information. And with the looming threat from Selene, the weight on my chest seems to be getting heavier by the second.

Blowing out a slow breath, I get up from the couch and walk toward the kitchen, where the warm, savory aroma of mushrooms and spices infiltrates my senses. I need a break from all the dark and heavy conversation. I steal a look at Gabriel, who is watching me from the living room. "You still owe me a cooking lesson."

He smiles, and the way his eyes soften makes my face heat. "I haven't forgotten," he promises.

"Good, because I'm going to hold you to it." I slide in next to Lex and lean over the stove, peering into the steaming pot of risotto. "Smells amazing."

He snakes an arm around my waist and tugs me against his side, dipping his face to kiss my cheek. "Yes, you do."

I roll my eyes, trying to ignore the way his touch sends my pulse racing. "Is it almost ready?" I hadn't been hungry before, but I can't deny the pang of emptiness in my stomach now.

"Should be." Lex moves away from me, humming under his breath as he walks to the fridge.

I turn around to start setting the table, and my breath

catches in my throat when I come face-to-face with Kade. "What... are you doing?" I ask, willing my heart to settle.

He tilts his head to the side, his eyes wandering over my face slowly, as if he's committing it to memory. The corner of his mouth curves into a grin that makes my pulse jump, and when he moves so fast my eyes can't keep track of him, I let out a startled gasp as he throws me over his shoulder.

"Kade!" I punch his back, though nowhere near as hard as the last time he pulled this stunt.

Lex chuckles from where he stands at the stove, shaking his head at us as if we're children that are misbehaving.

"What the hell are you doing?" I groan again, gripping the back of his shirt as the blood rushes to my head.

Kade walks toward the hallway, taking the steps upstairs two at a time, making me bounce against his hard body each time. "I thought we could play a little game before dinner." His grip tightens, making parts of me come to life far quicker than I'd like to admit—or ever will. He strides down the hall and kicks his bedroom door open with ease. Before I know what's happening, he dumps me onto his bed. My head hits the pile of pillows at the top, and I shake the hair out of my face, shooting a glare at him.

"I don't think I want to play your game."

He smirks at me from the end of the bed. "No? Your body tells me something else entirely."

I force out a laugh. "I don't think you're as observant as you think you are, Kade."

He licks his lips. "Hmm, say it again."

I arch a brow. "Say—"

"My name. I like the way it sounds when you say it. Almost as much as I enjoy hearing you moan it."

Heat flares across my cheeks, and I dig my heels into the mattress to push myself up, but Kade is there in a flash, pinning me down with his knees on either side of my hips.

My heart slams against my ribcage, both in surprise and excitement, and I lift my arms in a halfhearted attempt to push him off.

"Come on," he purrs. "You can do better than that." He grabs my wrists, lifting them above my head and holding them there in one hand. "You want to fight me off?"

Oh, hell no, but the thought of trying has me all kinds of tingly.

I swallow past the dryness in my throat and buck my hips, gritting my teeth when the only thing that accomplishes is making the heat between my legs intensify. "Get. Off."

Kade leans closer, and the warmth of his body radiates against my skin, the crisp scent of his cologne clouding my head. "Try again," he taunts, his lips grazing the shell of my ear.

"Fuck you," I say through my teeth, shoving with all the strength I can muster. He doesn't move a goddamn inch. Bastard.

He presses his lips against the pulse at my throat. "Don't rush me." His tone is laced with a deadly combination of arousal and arrogance. I should hate it, but instead, it has my core throbbing.

*Two can play at this game.*

Pressing my lips together, I lift my hips, grinding against him until his grip on my wrists tightens to the point it almost hurts, and he growls low in my ear.

"You're asking for me to flip you over and fuck you hard and deep."

His words steal my breath for a moment before I can force out, "Actually, I'm pretty sure the only thing I asked for was that you get the fuck off of me." I hadn't *asked*, but whatever. I tug on my wrists and attempt to buck him off with my hips.

Kade chuckles in response. "The sight of you struggling

under me when I can smell just how much you want my cock has me rock fucking hard."

Holy hell.

I shake my head, not trusting myself to speak.

He smirks, shifting his knee to press it between my legs, dangerously close to the throbbing there. "Use your words, Calla."

My head feels fuzzy, and before I can open my mouth and pray something useful will come out, the bedroom door slams shut, and I jump.

Kade doesn't move, save for the bit of hair that falls into his face, and the smirk on his lips remains in place.

"What's going on in here?" Gabriel's voice makes the pounding in my chest increase.

"Not much," Kade answers without moving his gaze away from me.

"Kade is being a total caveman," I shoot over his shoulder, trying to steal a look at Gabriel, but Kade blocks my view completely.

"I can see that." There's a tinge of amusement in his soft voice, and I'm not sure what to make of that.

"Are you going to help?" I ask, tugging on my wrists again.

"You or him?"

The breath halts in my lungs.

Kade finally rolls off me, revealing Gabriel slowly approaching the bed, his eyes blazing with liquid silver.

I scramble up the bed until my back is pressed into the headboard, and my gaze swings between the two vampires devouring me with their eyes. Inhaling sharply, I press my lips together. "Two vampires against one human? Doesn't exactly seem fair."

"We never said we were, angel," Gabriel murmurs, shooting

forward in a blur of movement and wrapping his hands around my ankles. He pulls me to the end of the bed until my tailbone reaches the edge, as Kade sits on my right side.

"You still want to pretend you don't want this?" Kade murmurs, watching me with a curious glint in his eyes.

Tension builds in my chest as heat flares across my cheeks. I want to turn my face away, but his gaze holds me in place while Gabriel's hands inch upward at an agonizingly slow pace. I finally lower my gaze, pulling my bottom lip between my teeth.

"You enjoy fighting us," Gabriel muses, sharing a look with Kade that sends my heart racing yet again.

"I..." My voice trails off before I can vehemently deny that. It's true. The taunting and the fighting—it's exciting. As much as I don't want to like it, my body craves it.

Gabriel's lips curl into the most seductive grin I've ever seen, and I'm suddenly frustrated I'm wearing pants, because his fingers are so damn close to the heat gathering between my legs, throbbing and begging to be touched.

"I don't know what you're talking about," I say, moving to sit up, to leave, but Kade grips my shoulders and pushes me back down.

"No?" he checks. "I think you're lying. To us—and to yourself."

I shake my head, knowing full well I absolutely am.

"You know," he murmurs, leaning down until his nose grazes mine, "I could always make you tell the truth." He exhales deeply, stirring the hair at my temple and making my skin tingle.

"Kade." There's a warning in Gabriel's voice, making me consider for a moment that maybe he's taking my side. Instead, he slides his hands up my thighs, curling his fingers into the waistband of my pants, and slowly peels them down to my knees. "I don't think glamour is necessary. She is soaked."

*Oh my god.* I want to hide my face or have the bed swallow me up, because he's right. I can feel the wetness between my legs, and it's for them.

I go to close my legs, but Gabriel catches them, his fingers pressing into my bare thighs.

"Keep them open," he orders, and his firm tone catches me so off guard, I do as he says, my eyes widening.

Kade lets go of me as he leans back, tugging his shirt off over his head and tossing it behind him. "Your turn."

I narrow my eyes at him. "This isn't strip poker."

"Well, of course not. Lex would be pissed if we played without him." He grins at me. "You can take it off yourself, or I can do it for you. Your choice."

"Choice," I echo breathlessly. "Don't get much of that around here."

Kade rolls his eyes, but they're still alight with amusement. "Especially when you take too long." He grabs the bottom of my sweater and pulls it up, forcing my arms over my head. It ends up on the floor with his shirt, and I'm left with my bare chest on display for both of them.

"I'm torn," Kade says, turning his attention to Gabriel, "between punishing her for misbehaving or ravishing those fucking gorgeous tits."

Gabriel drags his tongue over his bottom lip, then tugs my pants the rest of the way off before answering Kade. "Work fast enough, and you don't have to choose just one." He drops a light kiss to each of my thighs, getting close to the heat between them before pulling back and smiling at me with a dangerous glint in his eyes. "Something tells me she'll thoroughly enjoy both."

Kade hums softly, evidently in agreement. "As much as I'd love to punish you right now, I'm going to explode if I don't taste you soon." He presses his palm flat against my stomach, and instead of sliding toward the heat at my core, he trails his fingers up to my collarbone, applying a bit of pressure. Gabriel watches him, and they seem to share some unspoken words because, in the space of a breath, his fingers delve between my thighs. Kade drops his mouth to my breast, circling the nipple with his tongue as Gabriel traces his finger along my folds, so light it tickles.

I press my lips together to keep from making a sound, refusing to let them hear the pleasure they're giving me.

Kade sucks hard, and I gasp before I can stop myself, clamping my jaw shut and turning my face away. I press my cheek into the mattress, my pulse pounding as he continues sucking, swirling his tongue in circles, then reaches for my other breast, squeezing my nipple between two fingers. Heat floods through me, coloring my cheeks and chest a deep shade of pink as Gabriel teases me, dipping a single digit between my folds before pulling it back and skimming it back and forth across my slit.

"Gabriel," I practically growl, not allowing myself to look at him.

His finger stops moving, and he holds it in place barely inside me. "Yes, angel?"

I squeeze my eyes shut at his tone. He's torturing me on purpose. "N-nothing," I say through my teeth, and Kade chuckles against my skin, making me shiver.

Kade lifts his head, flicking his tongue over my nipple once before snagging my chin and turning my gaze back to him. "Liar."

I lift my brows defiantly and stay silent.

"Tell him," he says in a low voice.

"No—" My voice cuts off as Kade's glamour washes over me. I narrow my eyes, but I can't break his gaze.

"Go on," he encourages.

"I want your fingers deep inside me," I say, "your tongue after that, and then your cock."

"Good girl," Kade praises, releasing me and dropping his lips to my breast, giving it the same attention as the other.

Before I can snap at him, Gabriel inserts a finger so slow I'm going to snarl at him any second now. He slides in deeper, then turns it and presses his thumb against my clit.

I suck in a breath, gasping, "Yes."

So much for not letting them hear my pleasure.

Kade sucks hard, dragging his tongue back and forth across my nipple, and when I feel the sharp tips of his fangs brush my skin, I tense. He stops immediately and leans back in the same moment Gabriel pulls his finger out.

"Calla," Kade says in a gentle voice.

I shake my head, hating the worry I see in his eyes. "I… Sorry. I'm fine."

His brows tug together. "You—"

"I'm fine," I insist, reaching for him. I grab the back of his neck and drag his mouth to mine until our lips crash together. I'm not sure what it was about feeling his fangs against my skin that made me freeze, but the last thing I want to do is spend time exploring that. I would much rather continue what we were doing.

After a few seconds, Kade relaxes into the kiss and tangles his fingers in my hair, pushing his tongue into my mouth. I moan against his lips when Gabriel delves back inside me with two fingers this time. I lift my hips, urging him deeper, and am rewarded when he lowers his mouth to my clit, circling it with his tongue while thrusting his fingers in and out, quicker and deeper each time. He curls them at the deepest part of me, hitting a new spot, and my hips jerk off the bed. I break away from Kade's mouth, groaning as Gabriel continues winding me up. My orgasm builds quickly, and it doesn't take long before I'm racing toward the edge of release.

Kade peppers kisses along my jaw, down my throat, and across my collarbone, pressing against my side. I can feel the length of his erection against my hip, and I boldly reach for him. He sucks in a breath when I start palming him through the front of his pants. I fumble with the zipper, trying to get it open with one hand, while my other stays wrapped around his neck, and grumble incoherently when I can't make it work. He chuckles against my skin and pops the button, tugging the zipper down and pulling himself free. I wrap my fingers around his length and pump slowly, breathing heavily as Gabriel picks up the pace of his thrusts and sucks my clit into his mouth, swirling his tongue around it.

Kade steals my lips again, kissing me hard as I increase the pressure I have on his cock, and he growls into my mouth. My speed picks up as the tension builds between my legs.

"Fuck," he breathes against my lips.

"I… I'm—" My voice breaks.

"Keep going," Kade orders, and I'm not sure if he's talking to me or Gabriel.

When Gabriel adds a third finger and starts pulsing his lips around my clit, I dive right over the edge, my pussy clamping around his fingers as I cry out my release. The sound is swallowed by Kade's lips against mine, and I ride the wave of my orgasm while continuing to pump my hand up and down Kade's cock. His grip on me tightens a moment later and he growls against my lips, his release spurting over my hand, coating it in warmth.

Kade snags his shirt off the floor and cleans us up while Gabriel drags his tongue along my slit, tasting me. He presses his lips against my skin just below my navel and peers up at me. "Exquisite," he murmurs, making my cheeks flush as I try to catch my breath.

"Agreed," Kade says, kissing me chastely before sliding off the bed and walking toward his en suite bathroom. I can't help but watch as he goes. That man was chiseled by gods, I swear.

Gabriel crawls over me in Kade's absence, tilting my chin up to seal his lips over mine. His mouth tastes a little like melon, and a rush of heat floods through me when I realize I'm tasting myself on his lips. My fingers glide over his shoulder, and I grip the back of his hair, kissing him deeper, hoping he can feel how glad I am to be with him again. I fucking missed him—missed all of them. And I'm going to do whatever it takes to make sure Selene doesn't come between us.

## ❦ 13 ❦

# GABRIEL

Over the next twenty-four hours, a brand new, high-end security system is installed on the property. The existing one we had when the house was built was good enough until Calla came along. With recent developments, something more high tech is necessary. This system includes sensors on every door and window on all three levels of the house as well as cameras that cover every square inch of the property. Marcel also met with and hired a team of security guards to remotely monitor the feed constantly.

Between that and the four of us, there's not a chance in hell Selene will be able to touch Calla again. We haven't heard from her since Calla returned to us yesterday, but I have to assume there's a ticking clock on her threat against Calla's mortality. We'll kill Selene before she ever has a chance to get her fangs near Calla again. My stomach is in knots over it still. After being with Calla last night, I can't stop thinking about how we almost lost her. I would go back to Selene in a heartbeat if I knew it would keep Calla safe, but the others refuse to allow it to happen. They are confident she is safe here with us, but they don't know Selene like I do… The woman is deceitful and manipulative. She gets her way every time, no matter who gets hurt in the process. I've seen it too many times to count. I gave her what she wanted at the expense of others more times than I'd like to admit during my time with her decades ago.

I drag a hand down my face, cradling a mug of microwaved blood in my other hand. I've been sitting in the dark at the dining room table for over an hour now. It's long past midnight, and everyone else is sleeping, but every time I close my eyes, nightmares from my past flash before me, and I jolt upright, wide awake.

"You can't sleep either?" a soft voice says, and I look up to find Calla padding across the floor in her bare feet. She's wearing one of Kade's old T-shirts, and it falls just above her knees, hugging her curves in a way that has me shifting where I sit. With her hair tied up in a messy bun and the soft scent of her rose body wash clinging to her skin, I want to bury my face in her neck and hold her until the nightmares are chased away.

I shake my head, taking a drink of blood. "Are you all right, angel?"

She sighs, dropping into the chair across from me, and offers a faint smile. "Define *all right*."

My lips drop into a frown. "You know you're safe here, don't you?"

Calla bites her lip, glancing down at her lap. "Yeah. I just… How long until Selene's blood and venom are out of my system? Like, for sure?"

I tap my fingers against the side of my mug. I can see the concern on her face, in the way her eyes flick between mine and gleam with uncertainty. I want to take that away, reassure her everything will be fine, but the truth is, Selene is capable of far greater evil than I hope she—or the others—will ever know. "A few days."

She nods absently, finally looking at me. "Will you tell me about her?"

My forehead creases when I lift my brows at her in surprise. "About Selene?" I check, unease swirling deep in my stomach.

"Yeah. I mean, how did you meet? She turned you into a vampire, so I have to assume she was important to you. You're clearly important to her, so much so, she wanted to ensure you would live forever." She grips the back of her neck as she shifts in her chair. I don't like how uncomfortable she is.

"Selene cares about very few things, Calla," I tell her in a soft voice. "Back then, I... I thought what we had was love. I was very wrong. She manipulated me, glamoured me most of the time we were together, which of course I didn't realize until much later."

Her face is several shades paler than when she sat down. "After you turned?"

Nodding, I admit, "I didn't want to be a vampire. When I discovered what Selene was, I wanted to run. I was terrified. But I also cared about her a great deal, so I stayed. She was different then—at least, she made me believe that she was. Kind and gentle; she would never hurt anyone and would survive off donated blood, much like we do now."

Calla frowns. "When did that change?"

I inhale slowly. Searching through memories of that time isn't easy for me, but I want to tell her everything I know. Answer any questions she has, because after keeping her in the dark for so long, it's the least she deserves. "It wasn't all at once. There were small things here and there. And then one night, she wanted me to taste her blood. We had been..."

"Fucking," Calla offers.

I exhale a humorless laugh. "Yes. She had bitten me—it wasn't the first time, but the first time while we were intimate. With my blood still on her lips, she used her fingernail and sliced into her throat, beckoning me to drink from her." I close my eyes for a moment, shuddering at the memory, at how clear it still is all these years later.

"Gabriel," Calla murmurs, and a moment later, her hands wrap around mine. "You don't have to tell me. I can't imagine what you went through at her hands. If thinking about it brings you pain, I... I don't want that."

I open my eyes, dropping my gaze to our hands. The way her thumb is brushing over my skin eases the tension in my chest somewhat, and I manage a small smile. "It's okay, angel. You should know what we're up against."

She nods and continues holding my hands.

"I didn't want to drink her blood. The very thought of it made me nauseous. I tried to refuse her, I *did* refuse her. But she glamoured me; made me think I *wanted* it." I shake my head. "She may as well have turned me that night."

Calla's brows knit. "When did she turn you?"

"Not for months after that. I think she enjoyed being able to feed on me, but she also got satisfaction from me drinking her blood as a human, even though she glamoured me into it every time." I take a deep breath. "When she did turn me, I was angry and scared and confused. My body went through so many changes at once and everything was overwhelming. I didn't know what to do. I relied on her for a time. She was all I knew, so I didn't have much of a choice. I... I did a lot of terrible things I'll never be able to take back. A lot of people died because of me. One day, it was as if I just woke up. I remembered everything she did to me as a human—the pain she caused me and seemingly everyone around us. So, I left. Packed a bag in the middle of the night and never looked back. I had a lot of growing pains and relearning to do when it came to being a vampire apart from Selene, but luckily, Lex and Atlas found me not long after. Everything since then has been okay."

Her jaw clenches and her fingers grip mine with a surprising amount of strength. "Selene deserves to rot in hell for what she did to you." Her voice shakes with anger—anger that's reflected in the darkness of her eyes. There's also exhaustion there in the form of shadows under her lashes.

"Her day will come," I assure her. "Atlas, Kade, and Lex will make sure of it."

"What about you?"

"She's my sire, so I can't directly bring her any harm."

She shakes her head. "That's not fair."

I shrug. "No, but I know what needs to happen will. I've made peace with everything else."

Calla stares at me for a moment. "I've never met anyone like you, Gabriel."

More of the tension in my muscles releases, and the smile I give her feels more genuine and less forced this time. "I could say the same for you."

Her cheeks flush. "I really missed you."

I meet her gaze and pull a hand away from her grip to brush my fingers across her cheek. "That week you were gone was the longest of my existence, angel."

Tears gather in her beautiful eyes, making them glassy. "I'll try not to get kidnapped again," she says dryly with a weak laugh.

I chuckle in response, running my thumb along her jaw. "I hope despite what happened with Selene that you'll believe me when I say that we won't let anyone hurt you ever again."

She drops my gaze, licking her lips and sniffling. "I appreciate the sentiment, but you can't make that promise." She quickly wipes under her eyes before looking at me again. "And I don't expect you to. Atlas warned me that your world is dangerous for humans. I get it. And I'm going to do everything in my power to ensure my own safety."

My eyes lock on hers, and the fierceness in her gaze makes my cock harden. Despite everything she's been through in the last five and a half weeks since the night we broke into her apartment, she hasn't lost her fire. Pride fills my chest, and I stand, moving around the table with a speed too quick for her eyes to follow.

She sucks in a breath, swiveling to face me with flushed cheeks. "What?" she breathes.

I cup her chin, tilting her head back so she's looking into my eyes as my lips pull up into a smile. "I didn't get enough of you last night."

Calla's eyes widen slightly, and she bites down on her lip, making me long to do the same. To claim her mouth and her body as mine.

Without warning, I grip her hips and lift her onto the table, pushing the chair out of the way with my foot before my mouth descends upon hers. She immediately softens against me, leaning in and draping her arms over my shoulders. I tighten my grip on her hips, then slide my hands up her thighs, gathering the material of Kade's shirt as I go.

"Gabriel," she murmurs against my lips, and my cock twitches in my pants.

I bite back a groan; I want to take my time with her.

Pulling back just enough to see her face, I say, "What is it, angel?"

She pulls back and grips my forearms. "Should we really do this? Here, I mean?"

I press my lower half into her, stealing her breath, and the little sound she makes drives the beast inside me wild. "I'm not waiting another minute to have you. Let the entire house hear us." I claim her mouth once more, pushing the hardness between my legs against the heat between hers until she wraps her bare legs around me, digging her heels in to pull me closer. My tongue darts out and flicks along her lower lip until she opens to me, and I deepen the kiss, grazing her tongue with mine. Her hands slide into my hair as her hips desperately try grinding against me, and when she makes a frustrated sound against my lips, I can't help but chuckle. Leaning back, I murmur, "Tell me what you want."

Her fingers grip the back of my hair. "I *need* you."

A shiver trickles down my spine, filling me with heat as I look over her pink-tinged face. I draw one hand up to cup her cheek while the other rests on her bare thigh, and kiss the tip of her nose. "You have me. Always."

A hint of a smile touches her lips, making my heart beat faster. The things this woman does to me... I'll never get tired of them. "Let me rephrase," she says, "I need you *inside me.*"

I grin at her, brushing my thumb along her jaw. "Sounds like someone needs to learn patience."

Her eyes narrow and her lips form a pout. "Don't be mean."

As I slide my hand slowly up her thigh, her gaze softens and she opens her legs for me. The only thing keeping me from her sweet, aching core is a lacy black thong that I'd like nothing more than to rip from her gorgeous body. I kiss her again, softly, taking my time exploring her lips as my fingers brush along the material at the apex of her thighs that is already damp. I can smell her arousal, which only feeds my need to claim her. And when she moans into my mouth, pushing against my fingers, my control wavers, and I tug her panties down her thighs. She manages to wiggle them the rest of the way off, and they fall to the floor. I waste no time dipping my fingers inside her. One, then two, then three. Thrusting slowly to start as she breathes harder against my lips. My thumb rubs circles over her clit, making her legs shake, and I pull back to bury my face in her neck, kissing and sucking her skin as she lets out little gasps and moans.

When she reaches for my pants, I don't stop her. I need this as badly as she does. I pull back just long enough to tug my shirt over my head and drop my pants, kicking them away before stepping between her legs again. I wrap my fingers around my throbbing length, desperate to plunge inside of her, but I want to make sure she's ready for me. I run the blunt head of my cock along her slit, nudging it against her clit a few times and making her moan before I drag it back down.

"Gabriel," she breathes, her cheeks pink with warmth.

"I'm getting you ready for me, angel," I tell her, pushing just inside her tight little tunnel before pulling out and rubbing along her slit again.

"You're driving me crazy." She tips her head back, biting her lip as I continue moving against her, and my eyes go to her pebbled nipples through the material of Kade's shirt. I lick my lips, suddenly battling the urge to taste them. Her eyes land on me and she giggles softly before tugging the shirt over her head, tossing it behind me. "Better?" she asks, and there's a challenge in her tone.

"Much," I answer, pushing a little deeper into her pussy this time as I strum her clit with my fingers.

"Mmm…" she moans, closing her eyes and bracing her arms behind her as she pushes her hips forward to the edge of the table.

I pull back once more, adding pressure to her clit, and she gasps sharply.

"Please, Gabriel."

I lean in, capturing her lips in a fierce kiss. "You don't have to beg, angel. I'll give you everything you need." With that, I push all the way into her at a languid pace, giving her a chance to adjust to my size. Her pussy squeezes me like a fist, making my pulse tick faster as I force myself to hold still a moment. "Are you okay?"

She keeps her eyes shut and nods, but her jaw is clenched.

I rub her clit, trying to get her to relax a bit. "Talk to me."

"I'm… good."

I kiss her cheek, then press my forehead against hers. "Relax for me."

"Trying," she says in a shallow voice, and when I move to pull out, she grabs the back of my hip, holding me inside her. "Don't move."

"Okay," I murmur, brushing my lips against hers, and she immediately kisses me back. A few pounding heartbeats later, she slowly starts moving her hips, her breath hitching against my mouth, but she doesn't stop. She pulls back and kisses along my jaw, wrapping her legs around me and urging me on. I take the hint and resume thrusting, picking up speed as she clenches around me, making my head spin with pleasure.

"Lie back," I tell her, and she complies without question. When her back is flat against the table, I slide my hand up her stomach and between her breasts, taking a moment to circle and tweak each nipple as I continue thrusting into her.

"Fuck," she hisses as her legs dangle off the edge of the table, and I grin, moving deeper inside her.

"I've got you." I lean over her, finding a new angle that hits a particularly sensitive spot based on the soft whimper that escapes Calla's lips. My balls tighten when she clenches around my cock again, and her breathing quickens as she meets my gaze. Her lovely brown irises are filled with heat and lust, and the sight of her writhing beneath me almost does me in.

"Gabriel," she breathes, "I'm going to—*ahhh*." She presses her lips together, trying to keep her moans quiet, but I shake my head, pressing my thumb against her clit.

"I want to hear you."

Her cheeks flush a deep pink and another moan parts her lips. This time, she doesn't try to stifle it. "Keep… going. You need to finish."

I don't stop. "Calla—"

She meets my thrusts, tugging me back to her mouth. "Come inside me," she says against my lips, and her words send me over the edge.

I growl deep in my chest, spurting my release into her pussy as I thrust hard enough to feel resistance deep inside her tight channel.

Calla cries out, coming with me a second time, digging her heels into my behind to hold me inside her. "That was amazing," she says, laughing as she rests her head against the table to catch her breath.

Once the aftershocks of our shared orgasm subside, I pull out, my cock twitching at the sight of my release rolling down the inside of her thigh. "It was," I agree, sliding my arm around her waist and helping her off the table. She sways on her feet, but I hold her up easily.

"I think you broke me," she teases, leaning into me.

I kiss the side of her head. "Come on. Let's get you cleaned up and into bed."

She lowers her gaze, those dark lashes of hers fanning her high cheekbones. "I… I like it when you take care of me."

I smile at her. "I'm glad, because I plan to do just that for as long as we're bound."

Once we've showered, I carry Calla to my bed, where she falls asleep a few minutes after her head rests against my chest. I wrap my arms around her, holding her to me as I exhale a heavy breath, finally letting myself relax as I close my eyes and wait for sleep to take me.

I blink my eyes open, yawning and stretching my bare legs on top of Gabriel's plush black duvet cover. My lips curl into a smile when his arm tightens around my waist, pulling me against him. When I feel his hard length pressing against my thigh, I turn my face into the pillow, muffling the laugh that escapes my lips. Rolling onto my side, I shimmy back, pushing my ass against his erection with a mischievous grin.

Gabriel groans under his breath. "Calla," he murmurs into my hair.

I press my lips together. "Hmm?"

"You're teasing me," he says.

"She's good at that."

My head turns to find Kade leaning in the doorway, his wickedly muscular arms crossed over his broad chest. He's clean-shaven today and dressed casually in navy joggers and a black V-neck. Before I have a chance to respond to that, he struts into the room and flops down onto the bed, effectively sandwiching me between him and Gabriel. He yanks the pillow from under my head, stuffing it under his as I grumble at him, trying to shove him off the bed with zero success. Gabriel chuckles on my other side, and I roll my eyes. "Don't encourage this behavior," I say.

Kade smirks at me. "Wakey, wakey. Time to get out of bed, sleepyheads. It's almost noon."

Narrowing my eyes at him, I snuggle back into Gabriel's arms. "That's seriously what you barged in here to tell us?"

He reaches for me and taps the tip of my nose. "Nope. Thought you should know that I talked to your professors, and—"

"You what?" I cut him off, my voice pitching higher with unease. The idea of Kade waltzing around campus, *talking* to people I respect about *me*… I grind my molars, waiting for his response.

"They've all agreed to accommodate you finishing the term online."

My stomach sinks, and I suddenly feel claustrophobic between two vampires. "I don't want to take online classes."

Gabriel's thumb brushes back and forth over my hip. I think he's trying to keep me calm, but all I want to do right now is shove Kade onto the floor and yell.

What an infuriating, overbearing—

"It's safer," he explains, ignoring my glare.

"This is ridiculous," I mutter, shifting out of Gabriel's arms. I scoot toward the end of the bed to put space between me and them, then turn to look at Kade. "What will Brighton think? How am I supposed to convince her everything is all sunshine and roses when in reality I'm living with four vampires and her family hunts them for a living?"

Gabriel frowns and reaches for me, but I slide off the end of his bed and stand, crossing my arms. I'm still wearing Kade's shirt, which isn't lost on him, considering the lust-filled look he sends my way.

"You're overthinking this," Kade says with a sigh. "We can

make her think whatever we need to—whatever is going to keep you safe."

I blink at him, torn between the fluttering sensation in my stomach and the flare of anger. It's very confusing. "No," I finally say. "I don't want you messing with her head anymore."

He doesn't miss a beat. "Ask me if I care."

Heat rises in my cheeks, and I drop my arms to my sides, closing my hands into fists without thinking about it. "Can you stop being a complete asshole for two seconds, Kade? She is my best friend, and while you don't give a shit about her, I do."

Kade sits up, leaning against the headboard, and pins me with a dark stare. "Forgive the fuck out of me, Calla, if I don't feel the need to accommodate the legacy of our enemy. Especially at the expense of your safety."

"She doesn't even know about the hunters," I shout, my pulse kicking up—along with my blood pressure. "You can't hold what her family does against her. She has absolutely nothing to do with it!"

"This isn't up for discussion, angel," Gabriel says in a gentle voice. "Letting you go to school would be reckless with Selene still playing her games. We can revisit this once she's been dealt with."

My gaze whips in his direction, and I regard him incredulously. Of the four vampires, I really did believe that Gabriel would take my side. I shake my head. "And when will that be?" All of the warmth and pleasantness from waking up in Gabriel's arms has left my body, leaving me standing before them cold and agitated.

Kade and Gabriel exchange a glance, then Kade shrugs, which makes Gabriel frown. He's been doing that a lot lately, but I can't really blame him, considering he's got a psycho ex-lover slash supernatural sire trying to control him.

It's been a day since I returned from Selene's, which means her blood and venom are still in my system. She could still come after me and make good on her threat to turn me into a vampire. My stomach roils at the thought, and I exhale a heavy breath, snagging the guys' attention once more.

Gabriel presses his lips together for a moment before speaking. "Perhaps we can discuss the possibility of you attending classes, so long as Kade accompanies you."

My brows pinch together. "To every class?" As much as I would love to get back to class—to some semblance of normalcy—I can't help but recall the single lecture he went to with me. Of course, I have no idea what the professor taught that day, but I do remember how Kade played my body like a damn instrument. Thinking about him being there for every class… "I don't think that's a good idea."

"We can also hire more private security that will monitor you while you're outside of the house."

"You mean compound," I mutter under my breath. That's more and more what it feels like these days. I sigh. "Look, I appreciate you wanting to keep me safe, but—"

"My plan was far less complex," Kade interrupts, rolling his eyes. He turns his gaze to me. "The semester is pretty much over anyway."

"Kade," Gabriel says, "we're not only trying to keep her alive but happy as well." He looks at me. "Your wellbeing is important."

Kade groans and slides off the bed before I can respond to Gabriel. "You guys…" He shakes his head, walking to the door. "Pains in my ass."

I flip him the bird as he leaves the room even though he can't see it, earning a small chuckle from Gabriel. I sigh, resting my knee on the end of the bed. "This is such a mess." I understand their response to the situation, and appreciate how important my safety is to them, but being locked up, even in a house as nice as this one, is going to make me go stir-crazy. All I've wanted since I got here was normalcy. A sliver of my old life. And with this... I'm being pushed further away from it every day.

He offers me a sympathetic smile. "I know, angel. It'll be over soon, you have my word."

I manage a small smile in return. "Thank you," I tell him, "for caring about what *I* want."

Gabriel nods. "Despite how it may seem, Kade does as well. He's just worried. Having control over the situation makes him feel better."

If anyone understands that, it's me. So as frustrated as I am at Kade, I can appreciate that his overbearing behavior is coming from a good place.

⚜

After breakfast, I stop by my room and change into a matching black sports bra and legging set and tie my hair up before meeting Atlas in the gym over the garage.

He's hitting the punching bag in the corner of the room when I walk in, not stopping as I approach, though I know he heard me enter.

I steal a water bottle from the mini fridge and crack it open, taking a sip as I sit on one of the mats in front of the wall of mirrors and start stretching. I'm not sure what he'll have me doing today, but warming up is probably a good idea.

I'm bent over, my hands wrapped around my feet to stretch my legs when he finally walks over and acknowledges my presence.

"Morning," he grumbles, grabbing a water bottle and downing half of it before tossing it onto the floor where his hoodie and phone are sitting.

I let go of my feet and straighten, meeting his gaze. "Morning," I echo.

He jerks a hand through his hair and crouches in front of me, looking me over before he says, "How are you feeling?"

I blink at him, surprised at the question. "I... I'm fine. Better."

Atlas nods. "Good. Get up. Ten minutes on the bike at whatever speed and tension you can handle, then we'll meet back here." He doesn't wait for me to respond before straightening and grabbing his phone off the floor. I go from having his complete attention to not existing in the space of a few seconds.

I watch him the entire time I'm riding the bike. He is typing on his phone, lines of tension etched in his forehead. I want to ask what's going on, if it has something to do with Selene or the hunters, but there's also a part of me that doesn't want to know. Not yet. I need to focus on my training, on getting stronger and more skilled—so I can protect myself against the things I'm wary to ask about.

My heart is pounding when I climb off the bike and walk back over to Atlas. He puts his phone down as I approach and turns to face me.

"Everything okay?" I ask before I can stop myself.

Atlas hesitates. "No." He steps closer, his gaze darkening. "There's a vampire who threatened someone who belongs to me." He tilts his head to the side slightly, those liquid silver eyes flicking between mine. "I don't take kindly to that."

I swallow hard, my breath hitching when he glides his fingers along my arms before resting his hands on my shoulders. "And I don't take kindly to being repeatedly used as a pawn," I finally say, my pulse jackhammering when his thumbs brush over my collarbones. "So teach me how to fight back." I meet his gaze. "Please."

A muscle feathers along his jaw, and he nods, removing his hands from me. "Turn around."

I do as he says, exhaling a slow breath. When he steps in close behind me, I press my lips together, fighting the urge to close my eyes and lean into the warmth of his chest against my back.

*Shit, I need to focus.*

"Now what?" I force out.

"What does your gut tell you?"

"Uhh, right now, it's telling me to run." The urge to put distance between us is about as strong as the one to whirl around and kiss him, but I'm not about to reveal that.

"That's fair," he says in a low voice, resting his hands on my hips. "Your body recognizes danger. It has detected a predator and your fight or flight instinct has kicked in."

"So I should fight, right?" I say, a little breathless with the way his hands are warming my skin. "That's the whole point of this."

"When it comes to vampires, it's best not to run. But you already knew that. So if you can fight them, do it."

"And if I can't?"

He leans in, his breath stirring the hair tucked behind my ear. "Then you're most likely dead."

"Great," I breathe.

His grip on my hips tightens. "This training is more for your peace of mind than anything else, Calla. You won't have to use what I'm teaching you when we're around."

"There will come a day where that won't be an option, so it's important for me to learn, because if Selene tries to—"

Atlas spins me around to face him. "You don't have to worry about her," he assures me. "She won't get close enough to hurt you, let alone sire you."

The blood drains from my face at the thought, and I try to step away from him, but his grip holds. "Atlas..."

"You're scared of becoming a vampire," he comments, and the gentle tone of his voice is something so foreign to me, I finally look at him. There's no glamour behind his words, but I still find myself nodding. No sense in hiding it.

I don't want to be a vampire.

Atlas exhales through his nose, flicking his tongue over his bottom lip and nodding. "Okay."

"Okay?" I echo, my brows pinching together.

"It's not a discussion we need to have right now, Calla. Let's focus on your training."

"Yes, please," I say in a tight voice, trying to ignore the voice of panic in the back of my head. The one telling me to put distance between me and Atlas, to turn and run the hell out of here—not that I'd get far. The idea of eternity is far too big to think about without raising my blood pressure. I'd much rather focus on learning how to protect myself from being forced into vampirism.

"Good." He steps away from me, walking over to one of the cabinets built into the wall, and pulls something out. He walks back to me and holds his hand out, revealing a black leather-bound blade.

After a moment of hesitation, I take it from him with a frown, turning the sturdy handle over in my hand. "You're giving me a dagger?"

"It would appear that way." I want to roll my eyes at the mocking tone of his voice. Then he says, "The blade is infused with white ash."

My eyes widen. He's just handed me a rare, very lethal-to-vampires weapon. "Don't you think that's a little risky?" I ask him, tightening my grip on the hilt of the dagger, testing the weight of it in my hand. It feels good.

His lips twitch. "If I thought for a second you'd try to use this on me or the others, this would be a much different discussion, Calla."

I arch a brow at him. "What makes you think I won't? I've stabbed you before," I point out.

He wraps his fingers around my wrist, but instead of applying pressure to make me release the dagger like I thought he might, he says, "Are you planning to stab me?"

"No." The word leaves my mouth before I can clamp my mouth shut, the urge to answer honestly too strong to ignore let alone fight.

"What about the others?"

"No."

He drops my wrist, and the glamour falls away. "Until that changes, I'm going to teach you to protect yourself against vampires to the best of your ability."

I scowl and mutter, "I know what you can teach me next."

His eyes glimmer with a hint of amusement. "There is no way to resist glamour."

"Could be fun to try, though," Lex says, strutting into the room with a grin. He walks over to us and throws his arm around my shoulders, eyeing the dagger in my hand. "Oooh, pointy."

I roll my eyes and return it to the sheath. "What are you up to?" I ask suspiciously, shrugging him off me.

Lex pouts. "I'm bored, so I thought I'd come see what the two of you were up to."

"I'm learning how to kick your ass," I say, unable to help the grin spreading across my lips. It feels good to be taking control again—at least where I can.

He glances toward Atlas, who shrugs, crossing his arms over his chest. "Interesting."

"Are you done?" Atlas asks. "You're interrupting. So if you're not going to help, get out."

Lex keeps his eyes on me, pressing his lips together against a smile. "Okay, okay." I think he's going to leave, but instead he says, "I'll help. Where do you want me?"

I arch a brow at him, then turn my quizzical expression to my trainer. "Seriously? I can't beat you yet, and you think adding a second vampire is going to help?"

He shrugs. "A *different* vampire. Fight him for a few minutes so I can watch your technique from an outside perspective."

"I… All right, fine." I go to toss the dagger onto the floor, but Atlas moves too fast for me to track, catching it and shaking his head.

"You're never to take this off. Understand?" I nod, and he kneels before me, wrapping the guard around my thigh. My breath catches as his fingers brush my thigh, and I flush at how close he is to the increasing heat between my legs. I want to close my eyes and let the floor swallow me whole, because he can definitely sense how much this is turning me on.

Once the dagger is secured, he stands and meets my gaze, offering a dark smirk before turning his attention to Lex.

*Fuck me.*

Lex claps his hands together, and I take a step away from Atlas, sighing as I turn to face my new opponent.

"Keep your stance balanced," Atlas instructs from the sidelines, his arms crossed over his chest and his gaze focused on us. There's a dark determination in his eyes, but something else as well. Something that has heat swirling in my stomach at the intensity of it.

I manage to pull myself out of it and turn my attention fully to Lex as he circles me slowly, his eyes gleaming.

*I'm glad one of us is enjoying this…*

"What's your move?" Lex taunts, bouncing from one foot to the other.

I jump back when he jabs forward with his arm, his hand outstretched and reaching for me. "My move? To attack the guy who enjoys pain?" I offer a blunt laugh and dodge his second attempt at grabbing me. "You'll probably get a hard-on if I stab you."

He nods enthusiastically. "And then you'll be the one getting stabbed," he shoots back with a wink.

I blink at him. "Oh, Lex. It's a damn good thing you're freakishly attractive, because you sure as hell aren't funny."

Lex moves in a blur, and I don't have a chance to whirl around before he has an arm around my waist, hauling my back against his chest.

I scowl. "How am I supposed to beat someone I can't fucking see move?"

He leans in and nips my neck playfully, and I shove him away with another scowl. Of course, he lets me do it, otherwise his arm would still be locked around my waist.

Atlas rubs his jaw, glancing between us. "You need to anticipate the movement before it happens. You won't be able to move at the same speed as a vampire, so you need to learn to move first."

"Are you kidding me?"

His impassive expression doesn't change, but he leans against the wall, crossing one ankle over the other. "It's not easy, I recognize that, but it's what you need to learn at this… stage of your life."

I prop my hands on my hips, vaguely noticing Lex wander over to the barbells. "What the hell does *this stage* of my life mean, Atlas?"

"He's saying, if you were a vampire, it would be a hell of a lot easier," Lex calls out from the other side of the room.

Atlas shoots Lex a glare. "That is *not* what I'm saying." He turns his attention back to me with a sigh. "It'll take some time, but it is possible to learn. I wouldn't waste my time here if I didn't think you had a shot at getting this."

Now *that* I believe.

I nod. "Let's try again."

Lex appears in front of me, and I jump back, widening my stance to keep my balance steady, and duck when he swings his arm toward me. I kick out, catching his legs, and a grin spreads across my lips when he lands hard on his back.

"Keep moving," Atlas bellows in a low voice from a few feet away.

I fight the urge to look at him, to see what expression is painted on that chiseled face when his voice is that... strained. But I can't waste those precious seconds when I finally have the upper hand.

I slam my knee into Lex's stomach, pressing my full weight into him, then drive my elbow into his throat. He coughs violently, his face going red as he tries to pull air into his lungs. When I reach for the dagger at my thigh to show them both what I would do if this were any other vampire outside of the ones I live with, Lex manages to wrap his legs around mine and flip us over. My back hits the mat, and I don't have a chance to even attempt to roll away and escape before Lex traps my wrists over my head, his legs sandwiching one of mine, putting his knee dangerously close to the apex of my thighs.

"Fuck," I growl, my heart pounding against my ribcage as I glare up at him.

"You did well," Atlas offers, walking toward us at a leisurely pace, his eyes locked on me.

I spare him a glance, blowing the hair out of my face. "Look at me," I mutter, pissed that Lex got the upper hand so quickly.

Atlas's lips twitch, his eyes darkening with desire. "Trust me, I am."

A low rumble sounds in Lex's throat, and my eyes snap toward him, quickly finding the bulge in his pants. A flush fills my cheeks and chest, my skin tingling where Lex's fingers are wrapped around my wrists.

"What's next, coach?" Lex asks Atlas without looking away from me.

My eyes widen. He doesn't... He couldn't possibly mean—

"She clearly enjoys being held down," Atlas muses, walking around the mats as he keeps his eyes on us.

I scowl but I really can't say much, considering I've stopped fighting him. It's safe to say our training is done for the moment.

He drags his tongue over his bottom lip, a glint in his eyes that makes my pulse jump under his scrutiny. "I think she'd enjoy it even more if you slid one of your hands into her pants," Atlas says, his jaw set tight, as if that's what *he* wants to do instead of directing Lex to do it.

Lex's lips curl into a grin as he hovers over me, his usual scent of citrus and spice filling my senses as he switches his grip on my wrists into one hand, following Atlas's direction. Slowly, he drags his fingers across my collarbone before sliding them over my sports bra, down my bare stomach, and pauses at the waistband of my leggings. I'm pressing my lips together, trying to hide how my breathing has picked up, though it's probably more than obvious based on my heart-beat and the quick rise and fall of my chest.

"How wet do you think she is already?" Lex muses.

I narrow my eyes at him, my cheeks flaming as I fight the urge to look away or close my eyes instead. "Says the guy with a hard-on."

Atlas exhales on a short laugh. "Why don't you tell him, Calla?"

It's my turn to laugh. "Fuck off. I never agreed to take your direction when it came to *this*."

Lex glances over to Atlas, then back to me, cocking a brow. "I suppose we'll just have to find out." He presses his palm flat against my stomach and slides his fingers into my leggings. I'm wearing panties, so there's still a thin silk barrier between his fingers and the throbbing heat at my core, but his light, teasing touch makes my breath hitch.

"Hmm," Lex purrs, "you're soaked."

My muscles tighten, and I attempt to press my thighs together, but he stops me.

"Wrong way. I want you spread wide for me." He pulls his fingers out of my panties before tugging them down with my leggings until they're at my knees.

I suck in a shallow breath when the cool air from the gym reaches my entrance. I steal a glance toward Atlas, whose eyes are blazing with lust, though his jaw is clenched as if he's in pain. "What," I say to him, suddenly feeling bold, "you don't want to join? Too afraid you'll break me?" I taunt him with his own words.

Before he can answer, Lex crawls over me again and puts his lips to my ear, murmuring, "Atlas likes to watch."

I shiver at his words, then gasp softly when his fingers brush my sex, tracing along my folds at an agonizingly slow pace. He circles my clit a few times before going back to teasing my folds.

"Ask him," Lex says, looking into my eyes.

"What?" I breathe, hyper-focused on the teasing fingers inching closer to my entrance. My brows pinch together in confusion while my heart pounds against my chest.

He smirks darkly. "Ask him to let me make you come."

"I…" My voice trails off. I try to tug my wrists free, but his grip is impossible to break. I grit my teeth against the spike of pleasure when Lex presses his thumb against my clit and my focus narrows on Atlas as he walks closer and crouches at my side. Before I can turn my face away, he snags my chin, forcing my gaze to his, and stays there. Doesn't say a word, just waits.

Fucking bastards. Both of them.

I could refuse them. Neither vampire is glamouring me, which almost makes it worse. They're making *me* do this on my own. And as much as I'd like to ignore the heat gathering between my thighs and the tension coiling low in my belly, begging for release, I can't.

I hate that I don't hate this.

In fact, it's making me hot. I can feel my muscles tightening, trembling beneath Lex as I stare into Atlas's eyes.

"Let him," I say through my teeth.

Atlas tilts his head to the side slightly. "Sorry, what was that? I didn't quite catch it."

Bull-fucking-shit he didn't. The guy has supernatural hearing.

I narrow my eyes. "Let. Him. Make. Me. Come." I enunciate every word, my voice clear and demanding.

There's a challenge in his eyes that sends liquid heat straight to my core, then he says, "Ask nicely."

My nostrils flare. "Fuck you."

He tuts his tongue. "That's not very nice, Calla."

Lex pinches my folds together, and I gasp at the unfamiliar yet pleasant sensations rippling through me.

"Let's try that again," Atlas offers.

I stare at him for what feels like an eternity before I finally drag in a breath and succumb to his demand. "Let him make me come." My voice lowers to something just above a whisper. "Please."

I'm rewarded with one of his rare smiles as he releases my chin. "Now how hard was that?"

My gaze flicks down to his groin before returning to his eyes. "About as hard as you are."

Lex chuckles, moving his fingers over my folds, spreading them with his thumb and forefinger before dipping inside with a single, blunt digit, curling it in just the right spot to make me suck in a breath. "Right there?" he checks.

I nod before my head falls back against the mat, and I spread my legs as wide as I can with my leggings around my knees.

Lex takes his time warming me up with one finger before adding a second. They glide in and out with ease, and I moan, biting my lip to try and contain the sound. I'm not sure why, though this room does echo a bit, and I don't need the entire house immediately aware of what we're up to in here. Especially considering we're supposed to be training me to fight vampires… not fuck them.

When Lex adds a third finger, I press my lips together at the delicious sensation of being stretched for him, which only makes me wetter, letting him pump in and out easier. I start to close my eyes, but Atlas's commanding voice stops me.

"Eyes on me," he says. "I want to see your face when he makes you come on his fingers."

The tension builds at an overwhelming speed as I force my gaze back to Atlas and bite my bottom lip. My hips jerk, trying to push Lex's fingers deeper as I grind on them.

"Are you going to clench around his fingers?" Atlas asks, his voice thick with arousal.

"Y-yes," I breathe, my clit throbbing almost painfully. "Don't stop, Lex."

"No fucking chance." He picks up the pace, curling his fingers and rubbing hard against the most sensitive spot in my pussy.

"Make her come," Atlas says to Lex without taking his eyes off me.

"With pleasure." His thumb brushes my clit, circling it hard and fast as he pumps his fingers in and out at record speed.

"Holy shit," I breathe, almost choking on the air I pull into my lungs. My pussy clenches around Lex's fingers, and I cry out my release, my eyes locked on Atlas as my orgasm over-takes me. My legs shake, my heels digging into the mat as my heart attempts to launch itself out of my chest.

Lex continues his thrusts as I ride the wave of my climax, my hips jerking off the mat. I settle a few blissful moments later, the aftershocks rippling through me as Lex slides his fingers out and pulls my leggings back up.

Atlas shifts back as Lex gets up, hauling me up with him. I immediately sway on my feet, but he's there to steady me. After a few seconds, I'm good to stand on my own, and I take a step away to show him that. He chuckles, watching me with amusement in his eyes. My gaze swings back and forth between Lex and Atlas, my mouth too dry to say anything, because damn, that was fucking hot.

After our little, uh, *break*, we spend the rest of the after-noon training. I get knocked on my ass several times, but overall, I feel pretty good. I managed to stand my ground for a lot of the session, even for a minute when both vampires closed in on me.

Even when my mind wandered for the briefest of moments to the idea of the three of us doing something a lot more fun than training, especially with Lex's words playing on a loop in my head.

*Atlas likes to watch.*

After a quick shower, I stand in front of the massive bath-room mirror and run a comb through my hair. There's a soft knock at the door to the bedroom, so I tie the plush white robe around myself and walk over to open it, revealing a smiling Gabriel. The sight of him instantly makes me feel better. Until I'm quickly reminded how easy it could be to lose him.

I clear my throat before saying, "What's up?"

He holds up a white rectangular iPhone box. "Thought you could use a new one."

Taking it from him, I offer a smile. "Thank you. And I'm sorry for losing the other one."

"We found it, but the screen was shattered beyond repair." He shrugs. "It's no big deal, angel, so don't worry about it."

Ha. Right. We've got enough to worry about as it stands.

I reach for him, leaning on my tiptoes and pressing my lips against his cheek. "Thanks again. I'm going to get changed and come out in a minute."

Gabriel nods, stepping back. "Take your time."

Once he's gone and I've closed the door, I pull out the phone to find it already set up. I open a new message, biting my thumbnail as I stare at the screen, considering what to say.

*Hey Bri, sorry for the silence on my end. Everything is fine, but I miss you.*

I hit send, and a minute later, my phone is vibrating with an incoming call from Brighton.

"Brighton, hey."

"Hey, babe! Are you feeling better?"

I press my lips together. "Definitely. How are you? Have I missed anything good?"

She laughs. "Nah, things have been pretty boring, as usual. Nothing new. Let's meet for brunch on Monday, though. I miss our weekly date."

"Uh, yeah. That sounds good." So long as I can figure out how to convince the guys to let me go.

"Amazing. Listen, I have to run, but text me!"

Before I can respond, the call ends, leaving me with a knot in my stomach. Nothing seemed *off* per se, but with recent discoveries, I can't help second-guessing everything I think I know about my best friend.

I scour the cupboards and fridge, trying to put something together that is going to be relatively edible. I'm still waiting for Gabriel to give me a cooking lesson, but I'm too hungry for that right now. I settle on some chicken skewers I found in the freezer and start cutting up some potatoes to mash.

Lex walks in as I'm preheating the oven. "Does Gabriel know you're using his kitchen?" he asks in a teasing voice, leaning against the counter beside me. "Need any help?"

"Sure," I tell him, "I was going to make a chopped salad if you want to do that." Salads have always been one of my go-to meals. They're hard to mess up and easy to customize with a variety of ingredients to keep them from being repetitive and boring.

"You got it." He pushes away from the counter and walks to the fridge, while I resume chopping up the potatoes.

I suck in a sharp breath when the knife slips, slicing into the side of my hand. "Shit." I press my lips together and turn toward the sink to rinse the cut out, but Lex moves in front of me, blocking my path as blood drips onto the floor between us. "Lex—"

He grins at me, taking my hand gently in his. "Don't waste it." Lifting my hand to his mouth, he drags his tongue along the cut before closing his lips around it.

I wince against the pain ebbing around the wound and yelp when Lex pulls back abruptly, covering his mouth and squinting as if he's trying to convince himself to swallow something he doesn't like the taste of. Instead, he starts coughing, and I frown at him. "Uh, I'll try not to take that as an insult."

When his face reddens and he starts to choke, my pulse races. Before I have a chance to call for someone, Kade, Gabriel, and Atlas all rush into the kitchen. Kade moves to Lex's side, guiding him over to the sink, where he heaves crimson into it.

"What the hell?" I breathe.

Gabriel disappears for what can't be more than a few seconds, returning with a blood bag, which he opens and tosses to Lex. He downs it quickly, tossing the empty bag onto the counter, and coughs a bit more before straightening.

Atlas watches the whole thing with dark, narrowed eyes.

"Are you okay?" I ask Lex in a small voice, unable to ignore the pit in my stomach.

He clears his throat. "Never better."

"What was that?" I demand, looking around at the guys.

Atlas and Gabriel share a look before Atlas says, "Selene must have used a witch to spell your blood to produce an adverse reaction to any vampire who drinks it."

"Likely the same witch who created the barrier spell around Selene's home that kept us from finding you."

I press my hand against my forehead, fighting an oncoming dizzy spell, and lean against the counter. The thought of being manipulated by yet another supernatural is making my skin crawl. "What does that mean? Is it going to go away?"

Gabriel sighs. "Magic like this is tricky," he explains. "It won't go away on its own. The witch who performed the spell needs to reverse it."

"Or die," Lex chimes in. "Dead witch means no spell."

"Right," I say, shaking my head as I straighten, my head a little less fuzzy than a minute ago. "Or the four of you could just keep your fangs to yourself," I offer dryly.

Kade snorts. "As if you actually want that." His eyes snare mine, and the dark heat there warms my core. "Deny it all you want, we know just how much you enjoy being bitten."

I want to look away, to hide the heat flaring in my cheeks, but I don't. Instead, I say, "Whatever. We need to focus on the bigger issue here. Selene didn't get what she wanted. We have to prepare for retaliation."

"I'll take care of it," Atlas says in a grim voice.

My eyes snap to him as my chest tightens, and I walk around the counter to get closer, jabbing him in the chest. "I don't care how powerful you think you are, that woman is insane. You can't just—"

Atlas cracks a smile, stopping my tirade mid-sentence. "You're worried about me."

"I…" I clamp my mouth shut, unable to dispute his claim. Because damn it, I do care. About him—about all of them. "I think we need to explore the idea that killing Selene may not be the best course of action." Glancing toward Gabriel, I quickly add, "She absolutely deserves to die. If you ask me, she deserves far fucking worse, but she's connected to the hunters—at least one of them. We should explore that, get some answers, and then deliver her the fate she deserves."

# GABRIEL

Listening to Calla at this moment, I've never been more certain of one terrifying thing. I don't wish to live in a world where she doesn't live and breathe.

She is resilient and brave, and in the face of such atrocities as she's experienced since we came into her life, she remains one of the kindest—albeit sharp-tongued—humans I've met.

Calla is absolutely magnificent. Truth be told, her fiery attitude and defiance only intrigue me more, and the thought of one day losing her, whether it be to old age or something else, twists me up inside.

After the incident with Lex in the kitchen, I help her finish making dinner, and the five of us sit around the table in the dining room, mostly picking at our food. No one seems to have an appetite now.

"Maybe I should spend some time with Brighton," Calla speaks up, keeping her gaze on the almost completely untouched plate in front of her. She's pushing the mashed potatoes around with her fork without eating any; she's as concerned as the rest of us, making me wish we could've kept her in the dark a little longer. If nothing else but to keep her from worrying herself sick, which is where I fear she's headed.

Kade looks at her with an arched brow, but before he can open his mouth and say something almost guaranteed to upset her, she drops her fork onto her plate.

"Hear me out," she says in a firm voice, snaring the attention of us all. "We need more information about the hunters. I can get it. Brighton and I are going to have our regular brunch on Monday, but I could get together with her sooner. Maybe suggest a sleepover at her place so I can search for—"

"No," Atlas cuts in.

"Yeah, not happening," Lex agrees.

I offer her a gentle smile, sympathizing with her desire to help. A quick glance around the table tells me the rest of the guys are feeling something too, because as quickly as they shot down her suggestion, they're all staring at her as if she's the answer to all of our prayers. In some ways, she is. And her protectiveness over us is refreshing. It's definitely new, and it makes me want to steal her away and lock her up in my bedroom. I'd like nothing more than to keep her next to me in my bed and never let her leave. It's a shame we don't have that luxury right now.

"Fine," she grits out. "What's *your* plan?"

"There wasn't a plan, per se, for a long time," Kade tells her. "While the hunters want us dead—and have for decades —we just want to exist in peace."

"For the most part," Lex chimes in with a wink at Calla.

She rolls her eyes at him.

I swallow a sigh. "There are some vampires who are a danger to humankind. It is in their nature—*our* nature—to stalk and prey on the weaker species to survive. Many take pleasure in the hunt. It is because of them that we are all in danger of being hunted."

"That still doesn't answer my question," she says, flicking her gaze between the four of us.

Atlas clears his throat. "It's not a simple answer. Have we considered taking the approach of wiping out the hunters as they wish to do to us? Of course. But the thing is, they also help us, in a sense, by hunting the rogue vampires who are out of control and risk exposing our kind to the general population."

Calla frowns, seeming to run through his words a few times before she says, "So there has to be some middle ground. That's what you're thinking?"

"Not with psycho vamps like Selene running around," Kade grumbles before catching the hardness in my gaze. "Sorry, bro."

I shrug; he's not wrong. Selene is exactly the type of vampire the world would benefit from having hunted.

"What if there's a possibility of working with the hunters?" Calla asks, focusing on Atlas more than the rest of us. It's just as well—my head really isn't in the best place to be having this conversation. Not when I can't get Selene's voice out of it. Calla is expecting retaliation, and she's smart to. Selene is up to something—she always is—and we need to prepare for whatever it is.

"Yeah, that's not going to happen," Lex says. "Too many years of history there."

She crosses her arms over her chest, leaning back against the couch. "I refuse to believe that."

Lex shrugs. "That's your choice. It'd probably be different if you saw them in action."

Calla visibly shudders, and there's a dark pang of guilt in my chest, though I wasn't the cause.

"We need to stay the course," Atlas says. "We'll continue observing the hunters' patterns and what Ellis Industries is up to so we know which groups of vampires we need to alert to keep them safe. While Selene appears to be linked somehow to the hunters courtesy of Scott Ellis, they really are two separate issues."

Calla leans back, straightening in her chair, but remains silent. The tension in her expression is a clear tell of how displeased she is, and I'm a little surprised she doesn't push back more. She's never been one to back away from an argument—even with Atlas, who typically scares the crap out of most people—but she says nothing.

When my phone chimes on the table in front of me, my stomach clenches with unease, as if my body knows who it is before I even pick it up. I stare at the screen, gripping the phone so tight in my hand, it's a wonder it doesn't crack. The message staring back at me is from an unfamiliar number, but the area code is local. It wouldn't matter; the message is very clear.

*I've been alive long enough to learn great patience, Gabriel. However, that only extends for so long. Your time is running out. Come to me, or your precious human consort will pay for your mistake. I'm sure you've figured out by now that her blood is tainted. Keep me waiting, and I'll have it altered to be poisonous to her as well.*

I read the message three times before shooting off a reply. I shouldn't play into her game, but the anger in my chest pushes me to react before I can stop myself.

*You're lying. Always lying.*

Her response is quick.

*Perhaps I am, but we both know you'll follow my instructions regardless, just in case there's a tiny possibility that what I'm saying is the truth.*

A growl tears from me, and while Calla frowns at me with wide eyes, I stiffen when another message comes through.

*You have twenty-four hours, my love. I look forward to seeing you soon.*

I drop my phone onto the table next to my plate, making the water in my glass ripple. A few seconds later, a final message comes through. An address to a highly sought-after apartment building on S Street.

"Gabriel?" Calla's voice sounds muffled, as if she's calling out for me from the bottom of a well.

I blink at the screen before tearing my eyes away and forcing myself to meet her soft brown gaze. Her eyes are slightly wider than normal and filled with concern. "Everything is going to be fine," I tell her, needing that look of fear to disappear from her face. I never want to be the reason she looks like that.

Her lips turn down and her brows inch closer. "What did she say?"

I exhale a heavy breath, reading the text aloud.

Kade curses, while Lex slams his fist against the table, making the silverware clatter.

"Lex," Atlas warns in a low voice, then turns his gaze to me. "How do you want to handle this? Say the word, and I'll finish it tonight."

Calla opens her mouth as if she's going to protest that, and she'd be right to. We just said that killing Selene before we know what's going on with the hunters is likely not our best option.

The pit in my stomach grows, and I grit my teeth. I've done many selfish things in my life, but I can't bring myself to allow Calla to stand in the line of danger when there's something I can do to ensure her safety.

I clear my throat, forcing bile down, and everyone turns their gazes on me. Taking a deep breath, I say, "I'm going to end this."

Calla shakes her head. "Gabriel—"

"Enough," I cut her off in a sharp tone, standing and ignoring the look of shock on her face. The thought of hurting her makes me want to put my fist through a wall, so I clench my jaw and walk away from the table.

Kade calls after me, but I don't turn back.

My mind is made up. I won't let Selene touch Calla again —even if that means I'm forced to face the nightmares of my past to make sure of it.

❧ 16 ❧

CALLA

I'm getting to my feet before he disappears down the hallway, practically growling at Kade when he catches my wrist.

"Give him a minute," Kade says.

"Let fucking go of me," I say in a such a calm voice, it sends a chill through me.

His silver eyes narrow, and he holds on for a stretch of silence that seems to last forever. My gaze doesn't waver. I tug on my wrist, clenching my jaw to keep from snarling in his face.

"This is fucking ridiculous," Kade growls, turning to Atlas. "Let's just kill the bitch now. Let her think Gabriel is coming, and then ambush her ass."

"She'll be expecting that," Lex says, his voice laced with agitation; he doesn't want Gabriel to go either. None of us do. "But we need to find out what she knows about the hunters," he says in a level tone. "Whatever that meeting with Scott Ellis was about, we need to know." His eyes shift toward Atlas. "You know we do."

Atlas's expression darkens, and he shakes his head but

146

doesn't disagree. "Kade." His voice is firm. And when Kade releases me, I don't stick around to question the surprising turn of events. If Atlas is on my side, hell must be freezing over. That, or he's as worried about Gabriel as I am.

I hurry out of the room, jogging upstairs, not stopping until I'm standing outside Gabriel's bedroom. The door is closed over, but not shut completely, so I knock once and push it open, letting myself in. When my eyes land on where Gabriel is folding a pair of navy dress pants into a black duffel bag, I slam the door shut. He keeps his back to me, but I watch his shoulders rise and fall as he sighs. Fear and anger go to war inside my chest, making my throat feel as if it's closing in as I struggle to find the right words to express the emotions threatening to break me.

Finally, he turns to face me, his expression gentle yet sad. "Calla—"

"No," I snap, walking closer. I keep a few strides between us. "You're not going, Gabriel." I'm fully aware I'm not physically capable of stopping him, but I still need to say it. He needs to hear the determination in my voice.

He glances at the floor, sliding his hands into his pockets. "There's nothing I can say that will make you feel better about this situation. I'm sorry." He lifts his gaze, meeting mine as he closes the short distance between us in unhurried steps. When he stops right in front of me, my breath halts, and he runs his hands up my arms, along my shoulders, then cups my face, his thumbs brushing over my heated cheeks.

"Kissing me right now isn't going to make this better," I tell him, swallowing past the lump in my throat and willing my heart to return to a normal pace instead of the erratic pounding currently filling my chest.

A faint smile touches his lips, and he tilts his head, his eyes searching mine. "You're right. But I'd like to anyway."

My eyes burn, threatening tears, so I lean into him on my

tiptoes, wrapping my arms around his middle and skimming my nose along his. I don't want him to see the tears in my eyes.

Gabriel sighs softly and tips my head back, sealing his lips over mine. I close my eyes, melting into him, losing myself in the warmth and firmness of his mouth against mine. I grip the back of his shirt, clinging to him as if it's the last time we'll touch, because it very well could be. That thought sends me into a tailspin, and I put all of my anger and fear and lust into the kiss, pushing my tongue into his mouth and grazing his as his fingers slide into my hair and tangle there.

I allow myself to get lost in him for far too long before I pull away, pressing my hands firmly against his chest to push back. Shaking my head, I open my eyes and meet his gaze. "No. You're not going to distract me from this, Gabriel."

He frowns, pulling one hand out of my hair and lacing his fingers through mine before I can move away. "Calla—"

"What do you think is going to happen if you go to her?" I demand, fear clawing into my chest like razor-sharp talons. Knowing what she did to him, all the manipulation, going so far as to make him immortal so she could control him forever... It makes me want to scream. That, and use the white ash dagger Atlas gave me to end this whole thing. I'm not naive enough to think I would be successful in a fight against her, though I did manage to stab her... The idea of driving that dagger into her chest sparks something vicious in me that I don't particularly like. I'm torn between wanting to stand back while the guys take her on and learn how to fight her myself.

Gabriel tucks a stray bit of hair behind my ear with his free hand. "I don't know, but I do know what will happen if I don't, and I can't let that come to pass."

"I..." I bite the inside of my cheek, staring hard at where his fingers are wrapped around mine. "I don't want to lose you." My voice cracks, and I squeeze my eyes shut. This wretched feeling of helplessness is threatening to overtake me, and I fucking hate it.

He gives my hand a gentle squeeze. "You won't, angel. I swear it."

I shake my head again, not trusting myself to speak. I need to keep it together right now. If I let myself start to cry, I'm not sure I'll be able to stop.

With a heavy sigh, I pull away from Gabriel and drop onto the end of his bed, glaring at the duffle bag as he resumes packing it.

"You should be catching up on schoolwork," he says in a soft tone, and yeah, I guess he's right. Finals are in less than a month. I have assignments to finish and exams to study for, but I can't help but feel as though all of that is pretty minuscule compared to what's going on here. Gabriel knows how much school means to me, and I can appreciate he's trying to be supportive and leave on a light note, but I'm so torn between sadness and anger at our situation that I continue to sit there silently. School doesn't seem so important right at this moment.

Before long, he zips the duffle bag shut, tossing it onto the floor and sitting next to me. "I know you're scared," he murmurs, running his hand up my thigh, warming my skin. "This isn't easy for me either, but unfortunately, it's our only option right now. There are too many variables in play, and we need to have a better idea of what's going on with the hunters before we rid ourselves of that monster. And we need Selene to think she's getting what she wants so she doesn't come after you again." He angles himself toward me, cupping my cheek with his other hand, and guides my gaze to his. "And to protect you, I will do whatever it takes."

I pull in a slow breath, willing my chin to stop trembling. "You shouldn't have to do *this*."

He smiles. "You don't need to worry about me. I'm not the same man I was when Selene sired me. She'll think I'm there solely because she threatened you, but I'll also be figuring up what she's up to with the hunters." His thumb glides across my cheek, and he lowers his voice. "Selene and I may share a sire bond, but it pales in comparison to the connection I have with you. And the blood oath has nothing to do with it."

Leaning into him, I press my forehead to his, closing my eyes as I listen to the sound of our breathing for a minute. My breath hitches when Gabriel presses closer, gripping my hips and lifting me onto his lap. His lips trail along my jaw, peppering kisses along my skin as I drape my arms over his shoulders. My pulse jumps when the hardness between his legs presses into the heat between mine, making me throb. I turn my face so his mouth collides with mine at the same moment I grind slowly against him. He makes a sound that I think is a delicious mix between a growl and a groan, and lifts his hips, teasing me as his lips devour mine. Gabriel kisses me as if he's trying to commit the feel of our bodies moving together to memory. To be fair, he probably is.

When I moan into his mouth, something in him sparks to life, and he flips me onto my back, guiding me up the bed before crawling over me. I open my eyes just in time to watch him drag his gaze over me as if I'm a sought-after piece of art. There is something deeper than lust and arousal in his liquid silver gaze, and while it scares the shit out of me, I find myself reaching for him, needing him closer.

"Kiss me," I demand in a breathy voice, grabbing the back of his neck and bringing his lips to mine. They meld together, moving slowly as we explore each other. Reaching for the front of his pants, I fumble with the buttons, not able to see what I'm doing. Gabriel chuckles against my lips and pulls away. His knees press into the mattress on either side of me as he rises and undoes his pants. I reach for him again, but he catches my hands and kisses the back of each.

"I'm going to take my time with you tonight," he says in a deep voice.

My cheeks heat, and I stare at him as he tugs his shirt over his head, tossing it off the side of the bed before he lowers himself back to my lips, kissing me reverently. He slides a hand under my shirt, lifting it as he goes to reveal my bare chest. I didn't put on a bra after my post-training shower, and based on the way Gabriel's lips curl into a grin against mine, that was a good call.

I gasp into his mouth when he cups my breast, using his finger and thumb to pinch and roll the nipple into a stiff peak. Heat pools in my belly as he continues to work my nipple, kissing me deeper and switching breasts a few moments later, delivering the same ministrations. My head swims with pleasure and lust and… I want *more*. I lift my hips to press the bulge in his pants against my core and nip his bottom lip, hoping he'll get the idea.

Gabriel slips his hand away from my breast and moves it down my stomach, making my skin tingle and heat the closer he gets to my navel. His lips leave mine, trailing a path of soft, sweet kisses along my jaw. He kisses my temple, my forehead, each of my cheeks, and finally, the tip of my nose, all while his fingers inch closer to the throbbing between my legs. It's almost painful by the time he slides under the elastic waistband of my sweatpants.

"I'm curious," he murmurs, skimming his fingers along my pubic bone, making me shiver. "Are you generally opposed to panties?"

A laugh slips through my lips.

"Because we bought you the nicest, most expensive ones. A whole drawer full of them," he continues.

"Hmm," I say, my chest flushed with warmth as he peers

down at me. "And they are very nice. But sometimes bare is better." I flick my tongue along my bottom lip, dropping my gaze to his slightly swollen lips. "Wouldn't you agree?"

Gabriel's mouth curls into a grin. "Most definitely." He makes quick work of dragging my sweatpants down my thighs, sliding back to the end of the bed as he tugs them off all the way, letting them drop to the floor. He runs his hands up my legs, from my ankles to my thighs, and I chew my bottom lip as he slowly spreads them open for him, his silver gaze never leaving mine. The softness in his eyes shifts to something darker—hunger.

My heart beats faster in response, and I grip the sheets on either side of me as he crawls closer, licking his lips and dropping his gaze to my center. My entire body heats and tingles where his fingers brush, featherlight and teasing.

He takes his time, kissing the inside of each of my thighs before skimming his fingers back toward my breasts, this time lifting my shirt higher. I pull it the rest of the way off, my nipples still stiff from Gabriel's previous attention to them. He cups them in his hands, massaging gently as my eyes flutter shut and my back arches. I push into him, moaning at his skilled touch. My heart rate kicks up when his breath tickles my entrance, and my eyes fly open as his tongue flicks along my slit. Barely there, but enough to make my clit pulse with desire. My hips jerk, and he moves his hands from my breasts, gripping my hips and holding them against the mattress as his tongue laps at my folds.

I press my lips together, my chest rising and falling faster when he shifts one hand lower, circling his thumb around my clit while his tongue dips inside me, torturously slow.

"Oh," I breathe, sucking in a shallow breath as he plunges his tongue into my pussy. His fingers press into my hips, and I bite my lip, finding myself hoping he leaves a mark on my skin. I try to lift my hips again, but he holds me down, and the pressure of his fingers biting into my skin paired with the pressure and tension of him working his tongue in and out of me has me panting in record time.

He replaces his tongue with two fingers, thrusting into me a few times before adding a third, making me moan at the sensation of being stretched by him.

"I adore that sound," he murmurs, crawling over me once more and sealing his lips over mine as he continues fucking me with his fingers. "I adore you." The words are a whisper against my lips and they make my chest tighten.

I pull him closer, reaching between us to pull his erection free, moving my hand up and down the thick shaft. "I want you inside me," I say, rubbing the blunt head of his cock with my thumb.

He groans, closing his eyes for a moment before opening them and meeting my gaze. "I wanted to take this slow. Enjoy every bit of you."

"But I'm impatient," I say with a little grin.

His eyes glimmer, and he mirrors my grin, slipping his fingers out of my pussy. "As you wish, angel."

I guide his cock to my entrance, licking the dryness from my lips as he drags it along my slit, coating himself in my juices before pressing the head against my clit. I press my lips together to keep from moaning too loudly, and Gabriel moves to hover over me, positioning himself without haste. I run my hands up his chest and lace my fingers at the back of his neck, pulling his lips to mine to kiss him deeply.

Between one moment and the next, Gabriel pushes inside slowly, stretching me to accommodate him, his breathing almost as ragged as my own. He rests his forehead against mine. "Is this okay?"

My heart pounds against my ribcage as my fingers grip the back of his hair, and I lean back just enough to meet his gaze. "I want all of you."

"You have all of me, angel." He thrusts harder, hitting a new spot deep inside me that sets off sparks of pleasure.

"Yes," I breathe, my entire body radiating heat. "Right there."

His hips slam into mine, over and over, until we're both racing toward climax. My breasts bounce with each thrust and sweat dots my brow. My muscles tense, and in the space of a heartbeat, my pussy clenches deliciously around him. I cry out, my release slamming into me like an unforgiving wave as I continue lifting my hips to meet his thrusts.

They become quicker, his hips jerking as he pumps into me. Moments later, he grunts, squeezing his eyes shut as he releases inside me. His thrusts slow, and he collapses on top of me, his cock still filling me up. With a content sigh, he pulls out and presses a gentle kiss to my lips. He wraps his arms around me, holding me against his side and pulling the covers over our legs. I listen to the steady beat of his heart and fight the urge to close my eyes and cling to this moment.

"I… I can't say goodbye to you," I finally tell him.

Gabriel tucks my hair behind my ear, leaning down to brush his lips against mine. "You don't have to." He kisses me again. "This isn't permanent. Once we figure out how Selene is tied to the hunters, we can eliminate her. Doing that before we know wouldn't be smart, but I promise you, as soon as we know it won't tip anyone off, Selene will very quickly no longer be a problem."

I frown at him. "If I'd overheard more when she was talking to Scott—"

"Stop," he interrupts with a gentle voice. "You have absolutely no blame in this, angel. I can't stand the thought of you believing that."

Exhaling a shaky breath, I meet his soft gaze. "She wants you back because she's desperate for power and worried about her enemies, one of which being the hunters she's somehow in cahoots with. Nothing makes sense, but something about this has her scared. She's acting out of selfishness and fear, so please—I understand you know her better than anyone—but be careful. Fear makes people go to extremes."

He pushes his fingers into my hair, leaning in to kiss my forehead. "I will," he vows. "You can't get rid of me that easily."

I'm not sure how long we stay there, our limbs tangled with each other's, but eventually we have to move.

I slip out from the sheets first, grabbing my clothes off the floor and tugging them back on. Gabriel watches my every move, his cheeks tinged pink and his eyes filled with something that makes my chest tighten. He gets up and finds his clothes as well, kissing me slowly before we walk hand-in-hand to the door.

He squeezes my hand. "Calla—"

"I'm not going to watch you go," I cut him off, unable to meet his gaze. If I'm there, the rest of the guys will have to hold me back to stop me from stopping *him*.

"Okay." His voice is calm, gentle.

The grip around my heart tightens, and I reach for him, lifting onto my tiptoes and smashing my lips against his, hard and fast, before I pull back and open the door. Stepping into the hallway, I pause as if I'm going to say something else —I feel as if I should, but nothing comes.

I swallow hard past the lump in my throat and let the door to Gabriel's room click shut behind me. Tears blur my vision as I hurry down the hallway to the stairs. I manage to hold them back until I'm behind the door to my bedroom, but the moment I fall back against it, I crack, pressing a fist to my mouth to muffle the sound of my sobs.

# 17

## GABRIEL

The ride to the address Selene sent feels like the longest half hour of my many years. My pulse is erratic and my stomach is filled with nerves. I managed to keep it together as the guys walked me to the front door, but now that I'm alone—save for the town car driver behind the wheel—fear has dug its claws in me deep. Nausea fills my gut, and several times, I have to clench my jaw and debate telling the driver to pull over so I can vomit outside his car. I manage to swallow down the bile in my throat and try to focus on the quiet jazz music filtering through the car or the humans rushing to get home from work to their families. Thinking ahead, I called out sick to work before I left the house, not knowing how long this arrangement is going to last. I figure my flu excuse is good for at least a week.

Despite the unseasonably warm weather, the driver seems to have the heat on nearly full blast, making the churning in my stomach worse. I grit my teeth, finally flicking the window switch to crack it open enough to get some air. The driver either doesn't notice or doesn't care.

He keeps his eyes on the road, humming along to the music.

As I watch the GPS screen built into the dashboard, the minutes until we reach the destination tick down. The closer we get, the faster my heart beats. Despite my deep hatred for Selene, part of me will always have a sickening loyalty to her. I never wanted to see my sire again, but my blood sings as we round the corner onto S Street, connected to her on a level I'll never be able to rid myself of as long as she is alive. Until we find out what her tie is to the hunters and what they're up to, the plan to take her out has been put on pause.

My stomach drops as the car slows to a stop at the curb outside Selene's building. The driver shifts into park and glances at me through the rearview mirror.

"Have a good night," the man says in a polite tone.

I unbuckle my belt and reach beside me to grab my duffle bag, unable to voice a response. Without a word, I go through the motions of opening the door and forcing myself out of the car. Stepping onto the sidewalk, I close the door and walk to the front of the building, where a well-dressed doorman in a dark gray suit and hat, who appears to be in his fifties, nods at me before opening the tall glass door.

I walk inside with my duffle bag over my shoulder, my shoes echoing softly against the shiny white marble floor as I head through the empty lobby toward a bank of elevators in front of me. Everything is white—the floors, the walls, the reception desk. In the air lingers the scent of overpriced cologne and perfume as well as the faint smell of roses, coming from the tall vases around the lobby. The scent makes my chest tighten; I can't help but think of Calla's rose-scented body wash as I walk through the space. Chandeliers hang from the high ceilings, and yet, I still feel as if the room is closing in on me. I press the elevator button, fisting my hands at my sides when I catch the way they're shaking.

Stepping into the elevator, I suck in a slow breath and press the button to the penthouse, because of course Selene lives in the penthouse. Her tastes haven't changed. My eyes stay locked on the climbing numbers above the door, and when the elevator slows to a stop at the top floor, a soft *ding* sounds, and the door slides open, revealing a foyer styled similarly to the lobby downstairs.

A large set of white double doors with a gold P1 placard above them stands between me and my sire.

I close my eyes, taking a deep breath through my nose and exhaling it through my mouth. I force my muscles to unclench and step forward, lifting my hand to knock.

The sound of footsteps coming toward me gets louder, and a moment later, one of the doors opens to reveal an older-looking human woman with kind blue eyes and shoulder-length, graying brown hair. Her lips immediately turn upward into a genuine smile when she sees me, wrinkles becoming more prominent around her eyes and mouth, and she opens the door wider.

So, Selene still employs humans. Not shocking, considering they're easier to control and to dispose of when she's through with them. In the time I spent with her, I can recall at least three different human housekeepers. I'm not certain what happened to them, but I can guess easily enough.

"Mr. Simmons, please come in." She steps aside, gesturing for me to walk into the suite.

I clear my throat and force out, "Thank you." Putting one foot in front of the other, I enter Selene's penthouse, resenting the increase in my pulse as my eyes flit around the light and open space, immediately searching for her. She's here—I can feel it in the tingling along my spine and the pressure in my chest. It easily overpowers the connection I have to Calla at this proximity, and I clench my jaw at that, wanting to snarl.

"May I take your bag? I've set up our main guest suite for your stay." Her voice is soft and pleasant. Perhaps she doesn't know I've been coerced into being here. Though, this woman is loyal to Selene, so maybe she does and just doesn't care.

I hand it over silently, and she beams at me.

"You are a very handsome young man," she comments, taking my bag.

Choking on a harsh laugh, I point out, "You're far younger than I am."

Her eyes sparkle when she smiles. "Yes, of course." She switches my bag from one hand to the other. "Please make yourself comfortable. Miss Selene is finishing a call in the study and will be out to greet you shortly."

I follow the housekeeper through the entranceway to an open living and dining space, decorated in soft tones of gray and white. I walk toward the fireplace, the light and warmth beckoning me.

"Can I get you something to drink while you wait?"

I look back at the human over my shoulder. "Scotch if you have it would be good. Thank you."

She nods. "And would you like anything else? Perhaps a drink with some sustenance?"

*Is she offering me blood?*

"We keep several types in the house. Miss Selene's tastes shift every now and then," she explains, as if the need to have blood available to serve her employer is completely normal. I can't help but think this woman has been glamoured, likely for years.

My lip curls back, and I shake my head. "Just the scotch, please."

With another nod, she hurries out of the room, leaving me to the crackling flames. I brace my hands against the thick white wood mantle and stare into the fire, trying to convince myself that I'm going to get through this and get back to my brothers and our girl.

My entire body stiffens when she walks into the room. I straighten and turn around slowly to face her. My gaze starts at her bare feet, skimming over her black painted toes. She's wearing a floor-length black dress with a deep V neckline. I force my gaze to her face, and my lungs hollow out when our eyes meet, that damned connection sparking between us.

Her crimson lips curl into a slow grin. "Gabriel," she purrs, "I'm so pleased you decided to join me. I asked Beth to give us some time alone."

I assume Beth is her housekeeper. *So much for my scotch.*

I focus on the borderline painful throbbing in my gums, my fangs threatening to extend as an array of mixed, confusing emotions whirl inside me. "I'm here," I say in a flat voice. "Now I want proof that whatever magic your witch used on Calla has been removed."

Selene sighs as if she's frustrated that I ruined what she thought would be a happy reunion. "I've been in contact with her," she says. "Tessa should be there as we speak."

My eyes narrow. "You expect me to take your word for it?"

She arches a sharply lined brow at me. "God forbid." She lifts her hand, picking thoughtlessly at her black manicure as she says, "Text your boys. Check that I am telling you the truth."

I pull my phone out of my pocket and type out a quick message to Atlas.

*There should be a witch there to remove the magic from Calla. Can you confirm?*

The text bubbles appear a few seconds later, and I stare at the screen until his message comes through.

*Yes. The magic has been lifted. Calla is safe. Are you?*

Some of the tension in my chest eases, and I exhale a

heavy breath. Before I can respond, Selene appears in front of me and plucks the phone from my hand. She turns it off and tosses it onto the couch behind her, stepping even closer.

I hold my breath, clenching my jaw as she leans in and presses her hands against my chest. "What are you doing?" I say in a tight voice, my hands itching to shove her away.

Selene licks her lips, making the red painted on them shine. "It's been a long time, Gabriel."

*Not long enough.* I want to tell her to stop saying my name. Each time she does, the sound is like nails on a chalkboard to my ears.

She slides her fingers up to my shoulders and laces them together behind my neck. Her perfectly airbrushed face is so close I can count the lashes fanning her bright silver eyes. I used to be so enraptured by this woman, but now, the sight of her makes me sick. The monster in me may crave our connection created by my death, but I loathe her.

"A long time," I echo, keeping my arms at my sides. "What's your angle here, Selene? What are you hoping to accomplish by forcing me to be here?"

She laughs softly, her eyes alight with amusement. "Forcing you? Please. You could just as easily have refused to come." She lowers her voice. "Your little human consort would have paid the price for that choice, but make no mistake, my love. You had a choice."

"So did you when you chose to take my life from me."

She rolls her eyes. "All these years later, and you're still so dramatic about that. I gave you a gift. You should be thanking me."

Anger crackles through me, hotter than the burning fire behind me, and I grab her hips and turn us around slamming her into the wall next to the fireplace. Growling in her face, I snap, "You want me to thank you?"

Heat flares in her gaze, and the sound of her racing pulse echoes in my ears.

"Perhaps what I did was selfish," she finally says, her voice slightly strained. "I couldn't lose you, so I did what I had to do to ensure I didn't."

My jaw clenches and my fingers dig into her hips. "And yet, you still did."

She nods before cocking her head to the side. "I don't blame you for running," she murmurs, her blond hair slipping into her face. "I was born this way, but I understand how overwhelming becoming a vampire can be. Perhaps if you'd stayed—"

"Perhaps if you had listened when I told you I didn't want this," I cut in, my voice sharp, "we—"

"What's done is done, Gabriel. I'd say you've done exceptionally well for yourself. If you can't thank me for turning you, you can at least admit that."

My eyes narrow, and I pull my hands off her hips. "Why am I here?" I demand.

She purses her lips. "You know, Calla asked me the very same question," she says, sliding her fingers into the hair at the back of my neck.

I swallow my disgust. "So tell me," I implore her, "what are you up to?"

"Hmm, I'm keeping very busy with many things."

My control snaps, and I rip her hands away from me, shoving them down. "Things like Scott Ellis?" I shouldn't have revealed that Calla overheard her conversation with Brighton's father, but the words left my lips before I could stop them.

Selene laughs. "Oh, that sneaky little bitch."

My hand is wrapped around her throat before I know what's happening. "Watch your mouth," I growl in her face.

Her lips twist into an arrogant smirk. "You can't hurt me,

and we both know it. So we can continue playing—truly, I'm rather enjoying this hands-on side of you—or we can discuss the hunters."

I pull my hand back as if her skin burned my fingers and shoot her a glare. "Why was one of the most important hunters in the state here with you?"

She presses her fingers to her lips, considering my question. "We have a... mutually beneficial relationship—we have for quite some time."

Tension builds behind my eyes and my jaw aches from clenching so hard. "What kind of relationship, Selene?"

"Hmm," she hums, slipping past me and walking toward a hallway near the massive dining table.

I follow, my footsteps loud compared to her silent ones. "Selene," I snap.

She whirls around, her dress swaying around her, reminding me of the elegance in her I admired so long ago. "I think we could use a drink, don't you?"

"No. Tell me what you're talking about. Now."

She opens her mouth to speak, and I notice her fangs have extended. Despite myself, my pulse races at the sight of them. It's the same response Calla has had to mine.

"Very well," she says with a sigh. "I have a little arrangement with our hunter friends here in Washington and back in New York. In exchange for immunity from them, I hand over other vampires."

My stomach plummets, and I automatically step back, blinking at her in confusion. "You *what?*" I shake my head. She's turning in her own to our enemy—to protect herself. I don't question the need to... put down the vampires who pose a threat of exposing us to the humans, but I highly doubt Selene is making that distinction. No, she'd sacrifice anyone to save her own ass.

Panic lances through me, sharp and painful. We've

managed to evade the hunters for over a hundred years, and Selene has been turning other vampires over for potentially just as long.

The amusement in her eyes makes my stomach roil, but I refuse to look away. "I knew you were selfish," I say in a low voice, "but this is on another level. You were born a vampire—you have a birthright duty to protect your people, and—"

"Save it," she interrupts. "Your speech is about five decades too late, my love."

I stare at my sire in disbelief. "If I hadn't come, were you going to turn us over to them?"

Her eyes roam over my face before she licks her lips. "I suggest you go ahead and forget about that boys' club and pet of yours." She offers a victorious smile. "They won't be around to worry about for much longer."

Ice fills my veins, and my fangs split through my gums as I snarl at her. I advance without warning, slamming into her and taking us both to the floor. She manages to flip us mid-fall, and my back hits the hard marble, Selene landing on top of me.

"This isn't a fight you'll ever win," she says, bracing herself, her hands pressed into the floor on either side of my head while she straddles me. "Where's my *make love not war* Gabriel?" she taunts, and I see red.

Throwing her off me, I shoot to my feet and stalk toward her, but she moves behind me before I reach her. I whip around and growl in frustration, because she's right. I won't win this fight; I can't cause her any real harm. Which means I am effectively screwed—and yet, though I'm not arrogant enough to believe I have the strength or ability to overpower the sire connection that controls me, I don't stop. All of the pent-up anger and frustration I've been living with, trapped in a cage of my own making, rushes to the surface, and my control snaps.

Selene appears in front of me and doesn't hesitate before grabbing my hair and tugging my head to the side, exposing my throat. Her fangs sink into my neck before I can move away, and a strangled sound escapes my lips.

Strength flows out of me, and my legs give out. Somehow we end up sprawled across the couch, my gaze falling on the dancing flames as it blurs. The pull of our connection fills me with a contentedness that makes my heart pound, and Selene's lips against my skin transport me back in time to the many nights I buried myself between her legs as she drank from me.

I want to push her away, fight her off, make her stop taking from me just like she always did. Instead, I close my eyes, my limbs unable to move as her venom—and her decades-old power over me subdues my ability to resist her.

Finally, she lifts herself off me, pulling away from my neck and licking my blood from her lips. "I gave them up," she purrs, running her finger along the puncture marks she left in my neck. She licks the blood off her finger and gazes down at me, her lips curled into a cruel smile. "The hunters know where your house is. And they know Atlas, Lex, and Kade are vampires."

Fear cripples me as I stare at her, my heart in my throat and my vision dimming around the edges. "What the hell have you done?"

# 18

## CALLA

I allow myself five minutes to cry and then I slip into the bathroom, splash some cold water on my face, and pull myself back together. With a deep, centering breath, I walk back into my bedroom and suck in a short breath when I find Kade sitting on the end of my bed.

"You need to come downstairs." His voice is strained, and he keeps his back to me as I walk closer.

I run my hand over my hair in an attempt to flatten the mess I made raking my fingers through it repeatedly while I was crying. "What's going on, Kade?"

He stands and turns to face me. "We have a guest."

I frown, shaking my head. "What are you talking about?" I don't want to see anyone outside of the vampires I live with right now.

Kade reaches out and laces his fingers through mine, guiding me toward the door. "It's the witch who blocked your location from us and fucked with your blood."

I freeze and dig my heels into the floor. "She's *here*?"

He nods, standing in front of me. "You're safe, Calla. She's here to remove the magic from your blood." His jaw hardens. "Seems Selene is making good on her deal with Gabriel."

"I… um, okay."

His eyes search mine. "You trust us, don't you?"

I open my mouth to respond, but I don't really know what to say. I can't say yes. As much as I'd like to, the word won't form on my lips. But I don't necessarily distrust them anymore. I just… It's complicated.

"Okay, let me rephrase that. Do you trust that we won't let anything happen to you here?"

Pressing my lips together, I meet his gaze and nod.

"Good." He squeezes my hand, and we walk down the hall toward the kitchen and living space.

My pulse is a jackhammer beneath my heated skin, and the moment we step into the room, my eyes go to the unfamiliar face sitting on the couch next to Lex. Atlas stands near the front door, watching like a hawk. His eyes meet mine for a moment before moving to Kade. It's just as well, my gaze flits back to the black-haired witch, and when she turns to look at me and stands, my eyes go wide.

I'm not sure what I was expecting, but someone who looks to be close to me in age wasn't it. She has bright emerald-colored eyes that match the jumpsuit she's wearing, and dark, precise brows. Her pale lips tip up into a faint smile, and she walks toward Kade and me.

"That's close enough," Kade barks when she's a few feet away.

She spares him a quick glance, rolling her eyes. "Bite me."

I step slightly in front of Kade before he can respond. "Um, hi," I say to her. "I'm—"

"I know who you are, Calla," she says with another smile.

"Oh. Right."

"My name is Tessa. And I need to apologize. I don't typically get involved in vampire business. I'd warn you about what terrible company they are to keep, but I fear I'm a bit late with the warning."

I press my lips together. "Uh, yeah. Little bit."

"Right. Anyway, the only reason I agreed to help Selene is because I owed her. I certainly don't make a habit of getting into debt with anyone—especially the immortal type—but I didn't exactly have a choice. Selene saved my life years ago, so when she called in the favor, I couldn't exactly say no."

"Yeah, I don't buy it," Kade says with an edge to his voice and pulls me away from her so I'm standing next to him.

The moment I catch sight of his fangs and the darkness in his eyes, I move in front of him and press my hands against his chest, attempting to push him back. "Don't." I put as much force behind that one word as I can and hold his gaze.

For some reason, the moment I witnessed Selene killing Dante plays over in my head on a loop, and the thought of Kade doing the same to Tessa makes me go rigid with panic. If he kills her, he's no better than Selene, and I can't watch that play out.

Tessa sighs. "You can put the fangs away. I'm not stupid enough to come to a house full of vampires with a nefarious agenda. I'm here to remove the spell I cast on Calla's blood, and that's it."

I believe her. If she was here to hurt me, I highly doubt she would announce her arrival. Plus, I can't help but see a bit of myself in her. Perhaps if the circumstances were different, we could even be friends. I admire her fearlessness, especially being surrounded by vampires—including Atlas York.

Kade drops his gaze to meet mine, and I offer him a nod, hoping that's enough to get him to back down. His chest rises and falls deeply, and his fangs retract, his nostrils flaring when he returns his gaze to Tessa.

I hesitate before pulling my hands away from his chest,

and turn to face the witch, noticing the way Atlas and Lex—who is now standing as well—are watching us, ready to move and take her out at any given second. It's reassuring for me, but I can't imagine how it's making Tessa feel. "What do we need to do?"

Tessa slides her hands into the pockets of her black blazer and shrugs. "It's a simple spell reversal. Should only take a few minutes." She steps forward, then pauses. "Your boys aren't going to go all vamp on me when I touch you, are they?" She steals a glance over her shoulder, and her posture stiffens slightly.

"No," I say pointedly, looking between the three of them. My chest tightens momentarily at the painfully obvious absence of Gabriel. I remind myself it's only temporary and try to refocus on the current issue at hand. Blood, spells, magic. Right.

"All right," she says, though I don't miss the tinge of doubt in her voice.

We walk over to the dining table and Tessa and I sit across from each other. Lex and Kade take the seats on either side of me, and Atlas stands near the head of the table, though slightly closer to Tessa.

*I'm sure that's not intimidating or anything...*

She slides her hands across the table and flips up so her palms are facing up, nodding to them. "When you're ready," she says, "place your hands in mine."

I don't hesitate. Maybe I should, but the thought of getting rid of whatever magic is coursing through me is too enticing to delay.

Tessa's hands are soft and cool as she curls her fingers around mine and closes her eyes. After what feels like an eternity, she starts whispering under her breath—words I can't make out—and her skin heats against mine.

I bite my lip at the sensation, staring at our hands. It

doesn't hurt, but as the connection holds, tingles travel through my fingers, up my arm, and eventually start overtaking my body. I grimace at the discomfort that follows, and my pulse races, unsure of what the hell is happening to me.

The guys are tense on either side of me, and Atlas's eyes are narrowed on the witch.

A minute later, the tingling fades, and Tessa opens her eyes, releasing her grip on my hand. Her gaze sweeps across all of us, and she says, "It's done."

My brows tug closer. "That's it?"

She presses her lips together against a smile. "Yep. That's it."

"How do we know it worked?" Kade challenges.

I sigh, getting up and grabbing a knife from the butcher block on the counter. I prick the pad of my finger and hold it in front of me as blood beads there.

No one moves.

I turn to Lex, lifting my hand toward him.

"Yeah, no. I'm good."

"Seriously?"

Tessa laughs. "I'm guessing you tasted her blood while the magic was active?"

Lex scowls in response.

I turn to Kade next, who just shakes his head.

"For fuck's sake," Atlas mutters, walking around the table and grabbing my wrist. He lifts my hand to his mouth and closes his lips around my finger.

My cheeks heat when his tongue glides along my skin, and I quickly pull back. When he doesn't immediately start choking like Lex had, the others seem to relax a little.

I look at Tessa. "Okay. Well, um, thanks?" I cringe at the awkward tone in my voice, but I'm not sure what else to say.

"You don't need to thank me, Calla. You never should

have had to deal with this to begin with, so again, I'm really sorry."

"What made you decide to come and reverse the magic?" Lex asks, his eyes filled with suspicion. "Doing it in the first place paid your debt to Selene, didn't it?"

Tessa nods at him. "I didn't feel right about doing it, so having the opportunity to undo it wasn't something I'd pass up."

"Uh huh..." Kade mutters from my other side, clearly doubting her motives.

Tessa arches a brow, flicking her gaze between Lex and Kade. "Wow, you guys must be so much fun at parties."

I choke on a laugh. Damn. I like this girl.

The four of us walk Tessa to the door, and after she's gone, I retreat to my room. Gabriel brought up my studies before he left, and as much as I would rather be in the other room with the guys, formulating a plan to get him back, if I want to pass this semester, I at least need to make an effort to study. Plus, a short break from the supernatural is probably something I need right about now, otherwise my head is most definitely going to explode.

I sit cross-legged in the middle of my bed with textbooks open all around me, scribbling notes here and highlighting passages there.

I'm so engrossed in my sociology textbook that I don't hear the knock at my door or the sound of it opening. When I look up and find Lex leaning in the doorway, I jump a little.

"Sorry," he says with a little smirk, "didn't mean to startle you."

I snap the cap on my highlighter and toss it into the text-book before closing it. "What's up?"

He walks over and sits on the edge of my bed. "Considering it's well after midnight, and you're in here studying, I came to ask you that very question."

I purse my lips. "I lost track of time," I tell him with a sigh. "Finals are, like, next week and I needed something else to focus on for a little while."

Lex nods. "I get that." He reaches over and collects the books, stacking them on the table next to the bed. "You should get some sleep. Aren't you tired?"

"Honestly? No. I mean, I'm physically exhausted, but the thought of sleeping... How can I when I know where Gabriel is and *who* he's with?"

"Gabriel is strong," he assures me. "Whatever happens, he's going to be okay."

I glance down at my lap, unprepared for the sting of tears in my eyes. "You sound so sure."

Lex chuckles, wrapping his hand around my knee. "I've known him for over a century. I am certain."

I nod, still feeling at such a loss. "What are we supposed to do now?"

He exhales a heavy breath. "Now we figure out what the hell the hunters are doing conspiring with a vampire. Once we find out, we can send Selene to the depths of hell and call it a day."

I look up, raising my brows at him. "What?"

He shoots me a wink. "I'm kidding about the hell part. But once we find out what Selene was doing with your friend's father, we can eliminate her, and Gabriel can come home."

"Are you finally going to let me help then?"

"You are, Calla."

My eyes narrow. "That's not... You know what I mean. I can do more, and all of you know it, you just won't let me."

"Why don't we talk about that tomorrow? Today has already been a long one, and I think we could all use a quick timeout before the next period."

"Fine," I finally say. "And a sports analogy?" I shake my head at him. "Know your audience, Lex."

His lips curl into a grin, and he leans in, sliding his hand from my knee up my thigh. "Oh, I know plenty about my audience." His mouth traces the shell of my ear, sending shivers through me, and I lean toward him. He smells faintly of pine and soap and his white hair is still a bit damp from a shower. I trace the lines of vines across his arm while his lips find the delicate skin between my neck and shoulder.

"I want to taste you," he murmurs against my skin.

My pulse jumps, and I tilt my head to the side, offering him my neck. We know my blood is safe now, and the thought of Lex biting me has my belly pooling with heat.

"Mmm…" His tongue flicks out, and he snakes an arm around my waist. "Not what I meant, but fuck, you offering yourself to me like that went right to my cock."

Pressing my lips together, my gaze drops to his groin and my cheeks flush at the obvious erection there.

He leans back and pulls off his shirt before closing the distance between us and dropping his mouth to mine, claiming it. Claiming *me*.

Our lips move together, and I close my eyes, letting him take the lead. Lex guides me onto my back, and I stretch my legs out as my head hits the pillows at the headboard. We lay next to each other on our sides, and he deepens the kiss, grabbing my hips and hauling me flush against him. My breasts press against his bare chest, my nipples pebbling at the friction between him and my shirt.

Anticipation sparks to life inside me, and I can't tug my shirt off fast enough. I break the kiss to do it, but quickly return to his mouth, moaning against his lips when his hands palm my breasts. He uses that opportunity to push his tongue into my mouth, grazing mine sensually as my heart hammers against my chest. Heat gathers between my legs, and before long, I grab his hand and guide it down my stomach to the waistband of my pants.

He chuckles softly, pulling his lips away from me for a moment. "Something you want?"

"Thought I was being pretty clear," I shoot back, the tension coiling in me growing more intense by the second. I hadn't realized how tightly wound I was until he started touching me. And now that he has… "I need you inside me."

He steals my lips again, briefly, then meets my gaze, his own ablaze with lust. "I know exactly what you need, and I intend to give it to you."

Lex moves at a preternatural speed, curling his fingers around the waistband of my pants and pulling them off in a single, quick motion. They end up somewhere on the floor at the end of the bed, but I really couldn't care less. Especially when Lex is looking at me as if he's a death row prisoner, and I'm his last meal.

My gaze locks on his as he crawls up the bed, wrapping his arms around my thighs and spreading them without a moment of hesitation. He holds me wide open and presses a kiss just below my navel, dragging his lips down until his breath tickles the most intimate part of me. His tongue darts out, flicking against my clit a few times before he glides it along my folds. My chest flushes, and I reach above me to grab hold of the headboard, my thighs tensing on either side of his head.

The sight of him between my legs spikes my pulse, and I suck in a sharp breath when he presses his tongue flat against my slit, dipping into me as he drags it back up to my clit, circling it until I'm panting.

He draws my clit into his mouth, sucking it between his lips and eliciting a throaty moan from me.

"You know, some of us are trying to sleep." Kade's voice slices through the haze of lust, and my breath hitches as I turn my head to find him leaning against the closed door.

Lex chuckles, and I press my lips together, the vibrations against my sex making me squirm.

"Well, Atlas went to meet with one of our contacts in Arlington to talk about some hunter activity, so it's just me, but still."

I roll my eyes. "Can we help you, Kade? We're kinda in the middle of something."

He drags his tongue over his bottom lip, looking from where Lex is between my legs to my face. "I can see that." He pushes away from the door, walking toward the bed. "Don't let me stop you."

With that, Lex resumes lapping at my folds, alternating between rolling my clit between his fingers and sucking it into his mouth to swirl his tongue around it. Kade kicks off his shoes and socks and loses his shirt before sliding onto the bed next to me. He snags my chin, turning my face to his and slanting his mouth over mine.

I let go of the headboard and grab onto his shoulders, pulling him closer as my hips attempt to jerk off the bed. Lex has a tight grip, so they don't move much, and I writhe against him as he plunges his tongue into my pussy. My grip tightens on Kade's shoulders, and I moan into his mouth, breaking the searing kiss to suck in a breath of air. Lex thrusts his tongue in deeper, flicking it against my pussy walls as his thumb pulses against my clit. My entire body flushes as I race toward orgasm, and Kade reaches over and tweaks my nipples, sending me over the edge.

Lex glides his tongue out of me, licking up the length of my slit and devouring every bit of moisture there, making my cheeks fill with heat to the point of feeling slightly feverish. He crawls up the bed and lays on my other side, sandwiching me between him and Kade.

I reach for the bulge in Lex's pants, unbuttoning them to pull his cock free. He makes quick work of losing the remainder of his clothes, and without turning to look, I hear Kade doing the same behind me until all three of us are completely naked.

They guide me onto my side, and Lex grips his thick cock in his fist, pumping it up and down as I watch, biting my lip. From behind me, Kade kisses my shoulder, his fangs scraping against my skin and making my pulse race as I shiver in anticipation.

"Not yet," Lex tells him, shifting closer and teasing my entrance with his cock.

"I want it," I murmur, my cheeks hot.

Lex smirks. "Oh, I know you do. And you'll get it. You just need to be patient."

I want to scowl at him and protest that, but before I can, he pushes into me with one deep thrust, and I suddenly have lost the ability to form words.

Kade sucks gently on the skin between my neck and shoulder, swirling his tongue there as his hand slides over my hip and finds my clit, circling it while Lex increases the speed of his thrusts, gliding in and out of me easily.

"We're going to fill you up," Lex taunts, making me shiver. I'm practically delirious with arousal, so all I can do is nod. But when I feel the blunt head of Kade behind me, I tense, clenching around Lex's cock.

"There is no fucking way you're putting that there," I breathe. Even as I say the words, part of me wants to try it.

Kade chuckles, rubbing his cock between my ass cheeks, fueling my curiosity.

Lex smirks. "You can take it," he assures me, slowing his thrusts, but still going just as deep. "You just need to relax."

My brows pinch together as I purse my lips. "I... I don't know."

He nods. "Take a deep breath for me."

As I do, Kade reaches over and opens the drawer in the table next to the bed, producing a bottle of lube.

Heat rises in my cheeks and my gaze swings back to Lex. "How long has that been there?" I hadn't thought to look in the drawer, but there's also a rose gold clit stimulator and a matte black dildo.

Lex's smirk turns into more of an amused grin, and he pumps into me again, holding still deep inside. "It was your welcome package. Clearly I should have left it on the bed instead of in the drawer."

I roll my eyes, biting my lip when he hits a new spot with his next thrust. My pulse jumps at the sound of Kade squirting lube onto his hand. He works it over his cock, then teases my clit with his thumb and forefinger. I inhale through my nose, then exhale through my mouth as he pushes an inch into my ass.

The pressure is the most intense thing I've felt in my life, and I grab onto Lex's shoulder to steady myself, squeezing my eyes shut as I will my muscles not to lock up.

"Keep breathing," he murmurs.

I drag in another shallow breath, letting it out slowly.

Kade pushes in further, rubbing his other hand up and down my back soothingly. "Good girl," he murmurs from behind me, his voice thick with arousal.

Lex slows the speed of his thrusts into my pussy, and my walls clench around him, making him and Kade both groan as Kade pushes deeper into my ass.

"Fuck," I grit out, tensing before I can stop myself.

"Easy," Kade says, gripping my hip to keep me in place, holding his cock still in my ass.

"Look at me," Lex says in a soft tone, and when I open my

eyes and meet his silver gaze, my world narrows on him and the tension in my muscles ebbs away, allowing Kade to push in the rest of the way. "That a girl. You're doing so good taking him."

"Holy fuck," I breathe.

Kade starts to pull out, and I grab behind me, holding him there. He chuckles, pushing back in, increasing the burning pressure. "You're driving me crazy," he says against my hair.

"You're literally fucking my ass. Give me a damn minute," I growl breathlessly.

He kisses my neck. "Take your time."

I blow out a breath and seal my lips over Lex's as he continues his gentle thrusts. I grip his shoulder tightly as Kade starts moving again. He starts slow, pulling out an inch and pushing back in, until my muscles loosen up. Eventually, the burning fades, replaced by a pleasant fullness as his thrusts pick up speed.

Before long, everything tightens, and I'm launched over the edge, coming hard on Lex's cock. The muscles in my feet spasm, making my toes curl into the sheets as I cry out my release, my pussy clenching around his thickness.

Lex manages to flip all of us so Kade's back is pressed into the mattress with me laying on top of him, his cock buried deep in my ass, while Lex braces himself on top.

He pounds into me, pushing me deeper onto Kade's cock as he lies beneath me, lifting his hips in time with Lex's thrusts. I bite my lip so hard, I taste blood, and both vampires growl as I moan loudly, making no attempt to hold back.

Lex's movements inside me become short and quick. He grunts, thrusting one final time, then throws his head back, his deep groan filling the room as he fills me. He falls onto the bed next to me and sighs contentedly, a sheen of sweat dotting his brow.

Before I have a chance to catch my breath, Kade plunges

his cock deeper into my ass as he reaches around to strum my clit with expert precision. I moan deeply while his mouth trails along my shoulder, and Lex reaches over to move my hair out of his way. As Kade gets closer to my neck, my heart beats against my ribcage, practically shouting at him to bite me.

Seconds later, his fangs sink into my neck, causing another orgasm to whip through me, and I announce my release with an uneven moan.

He pulls away from my neck, leaving the wound open as he continues pumping in and out of me, and Lex's fangs quickly replace his. The sensation of blood flowing out of me paired with the dizzying pleasure makes me feel as if I'm going to float away.

Kade curses darkly, picking up speed once more. A few more thrusts, and he grunts loudly, spilling into me. After a moment, he pulls out slowly, making me shiver as he shifts from under me, tucking against my other side while Lex drags his tongue over the puncture marks, healing them.

The room is filled with the smell of sex and our combined shallow breathing. Lex wraps his arm around my waist, pulling my back against his front, and I in turn pull Kade close, resting my head on his chest while he runs his hand over my hair, kissing my forehead. My eyes flutter shut of their own volition and my breaths slowly even out.

☙❧

I don't remember falling asleep, but when I open my eyes, daylight streams in through the wall of windows across the room. Lex is still asleep on one side of me, and Kade is on the other. I ache in the most delicious way, my lips curling into a smile as I close my eyes to steal a few more minutes of rest.

Before I can doze off, the chime of both Kade's and Lex's

phones wake them, disturbing me as well. We all sit up as they reach for their phones.

"Security system," Lex grumbles, his voice thick with sleep, and slides out of the bed. I can't help but admire his bare ass as he walks to the end of the bed and retrieves his pants.

Kade has the same idea and gets dressed as well, tossing Lex his shirt. With a sigh, I get up too, walking around to my closet and grabbing a navy knit sweater and plain black leggings. I quickly pull them on before opening my underwear drawer and wrapping my fingers around the dagger Atlas gave me. His deep voice echoes in my head.

*You're never to take this off.*

And I don't. Well, except when I go to bed—though I bet Lex would have found a creative way to use it last night.

I shake my head at the thought and secure it to my thigh before walking back to the bedroom.

The three of us head down the hall to meet Atlas in the kitchen, where he grabs a tablet off the counter and taps the screen several times before looking up. He glances between us, and then the three of them start toward the front door. Atlas must've seen something on the security feed outside.

I rush to catch up to them, shoving my feet into the shoes I left near the door before stepping onto the small concrete porch, leaving the door open behind me in case the need for a quick retreat arises.

There's a woman standing in the middle of the lawn, her black hair blowing in the gentle morning breeze. She looks eerily familiar, though I can't place her, which makes it even more confusing that she's here. As is the silver of her eyes— she's a vampire.

I walk down the few concrete steps and join the guys facing off with the woman. "I—" My voice gets caught in my throat when I look at Kade. His face has gone white as a ghost, and the others are tense where they stand on either side of him.

"Calla, go—" Lex starts.

"Who is that?" I ask, cutting him off.

"She… she's my sister," Kade forces out, his voice strained.

My brows knit when the vampire steps forward, offering a fanged smirk as her eyes sweep across the vampires in front of her before focusing on Kade. "Long time no see, baby bro."

Before Kade or the others can respond, a sharp growl of pain fills the air.

My eyes go wide as she steps away from Kade, leaving the blunt end of a dagger sticking out of his chest before disappearing into the trees at the side of the property, Lex snarling and moving in a blur to go after her.

Kade's silver gaze meets mine, and for the briefest of moments, I see fear in his eyes. He blinks at me, then crumples to the ground as Atlas moves to catch him, and a scream tears its way up my throat.

END OF BOOK TWO

READ BOOK THREE NOW!
mybook.to/entangledinscarlet!

If you enjoyed *Tempted by Fire*, please leave a review on Amazon and Goodreads. Reviews are so important for authors to find new readers!

Sign up for the newsletter at www.authorjacarter.com/ newsletter-sign-up for book news!

Join J.A. Carter on Patreon at www.patreon.com/ authorjacarter for exclusive access to signed paperbacks, bonus content, early cover reveals and book releases, plus so much more!

Follow J.A. Carter on Instagram and TikTok (@authorjacarter) to stay up to date with all of the things!

Join J.A. Carter's Reader Lounge on Facebook for first looks and exclusives!

# ACKNOWLEDGMENTS

To my amazing friends and family. Your continued support keeps me going on the days when writing is more work than fun.

To my insanely talented cover designer, Keylin Rivers, I am so happy to be working with you on this series and can't wait to work with you more in the future!

To my incredible beta team: Haileigh, Lindsay, Jennifer, and Allison, because you are all just the best! Thank you for your excitement surrounding this book, your insightful feedback, and your willingness to read on a crazy schedule!

And to my lovely readers. Holy shit, y'all. You really showed up for this story, and I could not be more grateful. I can't wait for you to read what happens next!

xx,
    J.A. Carter